Tainted

Innocence

He grabbed my waist and pulled me down into his lap. "Do I have to fuck you in front of your brother? Is that what it will take to prove that you're mine?"

"So, you would blackmail me?" I asked him in shock.

"It's not blackmail, Athena. You signed a contract with me. It's over when I say that it's over. Now, stop wasting my time and go get dressed before I bend you over this desk."

Marsha Official

(Marsha Osborne)

ISBN: 9798674526520

Athena

I stared at my reflection in the mirror and smiled. My name is Athena Vintalli, I am seventeen years old, and I am a senior at Bayside high school. I'm mixed with Asian and Italian. I am 5'5 with a petite body frame. I have small curves but not anything that stands out. My big brown eyes are something that I get from my mother, which makes me lucky. My long black hair reached my waist because I didn't believe in cutting it. I love to dance, and I am trying to compete in the big dance tournament coming up with my crew. My brother is Roman Vintalli, he wants me to be all about business. He is the biggest mafia leader in New York City besides Vain Grey. They are constantly at war with each other, but I could care less. I rolled my eyes when I heard him calling my name. I knew that he was going to lecture me about being late. I grabbed my backpack and ran downstairs quickly. He stood at the bottom of the stairs with his arms crossed over his chest. I rolled my eyes and walked past him because I didn't feel like hearing him lecture me. He followed me into the kitchen, and I smiled grabbing a piece of toast. I sat at the table, and he raised an eyebrow at me. My brother Roman was famous with the ladies. He was about 6ft tall, and he took after father. His baby blue eyes didn't have a sparkle in them because he was always angry. At the moment his black hair that he usually kept neat was a mess on top of his head.

"Do you know what I'm going to say?"

I nodded my head giggling, "yes. I wouldn't have to hear you lecture me if mom and dad were still alive."

He sighed running his hand through his hair, "well they are not."

My mother and father died when I was fifteen in a car accident. My brother doesn't feel like it was much of an accident, but that is him just being paranoid. My father was the leader of the mafia but then when he died it got passed down to my brother.

I looked down at the watch on my wrist and gasped, "I have to go. I'll see you after school. Don't wait for me because I will be practicing with my dance crew."

"Athena, we talked about this. I don't want you dancing because it's pointless. And I told you before that your skirt is way too short."

I placed my hand on my hip, "it's not. You wouldn't think that way if you actually came out and saw me dance." I placed my hand on my skirt, "my skirt is fine."

He put his hand up, "I'm not about to argue with you. Go to school and I will see you later."

I rolled my eyes and slammed the door. He was always so difficult for no reason, and I hated that. He knew that dancing was my passion and yet he knocked it as if it was nothing.

Sometimes I hated him, I hated to say that, but it was true. I picked up a flower and inhaled its fresh scent. Spring was always filled with so many different color flowers. If I had to pick my favorite season it would be spring. I placed the flower in my hair and bit my lip softly. I wasn't going to rush to school today. I looked up and sighed seeing the for-sale sign in front of this old building. I wanted this space to be mine because it would be a great place to practice. I talked to my brother about it multiple times, but he just kept telling me no. The owner wanted fifteen thousand dollars for it, and I knew that I would never have that kind of money. I stopped and placed my hand on the window peeking in. If only a miracle would happen, but this was real life.

"Are you still thinking about getting this?"

I turned around and placed my hand on my heart, "ugh you scared me Tarma."

Tarma is my best friend. We have been friends since we were in Middle school. She was 5'6 and had the perfect body. Her body had curves in all the right places and that attracted a lot of men. She had big brown eyes just like me and long black curly hair that reached her middle back. I always told her that she had the perfect tan because of her skin tone. She was mixed with Mexican and African American. She was sweet but could be stubborn at times.

She giggled and shoved me playfully, "come on you've been looking at this place for two months. Your brother won't pay for it so why keep looking?"

I shrugged, "because you never give up on your dreams. I swear I will come up with a way to get this so we can use it for our dance studio."

"Well, while you're thinking let's go because we are going to be late." She grabbed my hand and pulled me along.

I took one last look at the building before giving in and allowing her to pull me away. I knew that it was out of my reach because I didn't have any money, but I had to remain positive. I glanced up at the sky and smiled. Dreams do come true you just have to believe.

"You know what tonight is right?"

I looked over at Tarma and shook my head, "what is going on tonight?"

"There's this big party at the club downtown. You have to come because you would be lame if you didn't." She flipped her hair and smiled at me.

"Mm, I don't know about that. Roman would kill me besides, we have dance practice after school. We have to get ready because our performance has to be perfect if we want to make it into the next round."

She rolled her eyes, "you're all about business. Take a break sometimes Athena, it wouldn't kill you. Just come, it will be fun. You might meet a super-hot guy and lose your virginity." She giggled pulling me into a hug.

I sighed, "no. I'm saying no to the virginity part by the way. Besides, what would I tell my brother?"

"Just tell him that you are staying the night with me. I'm sure he wouldn't mind."

I cleared my throat, "I'll send him a quick text

and see if it's okay."

"Come on your brother is the leader of the biggest mafia group in this city. He is a busy man and I'm sure that he wouldn't question it."

I looked both ways before crossing the street and sighed. "I mean that is true, but I hate lying to him. You don't know what he is like when he is angry. Besides ever since our parents died, he keeps me close to him."

She stopped walking and grabbed my hand, "nothing will happen to you. I promise you that I will stay by your side the whole time."

"Fine, I'll go," I mumbled. She laughed and jumped up and down screaming yes. I grabbed her hand and pulled her towards the school. I could hear the bell ringing and the last thing I needed to do was to show up late.

I stared at my reflection in the compact mirror

that I had in my purse. I didn't even look like myself because of all the makeup that Tarma had caked on my face. I looked much older than I was, which was a bonus because we needed to get into the club. I tugged the dress down a little bit more to try and cover my body because it was very revealing. It was a mid-thigh short blue dress. There were no straps on the dress at all and my breasts looked bigger due to the strapless bra I had on. I looked down at the matching blue heels that were given to me and sighed. This was going to be a long night; I just had a feeling. The line to the club was long but that didn't stop my best friend. She was eager to jump into the line and wait. The name of the club was called Grey and I had never heard of it. It was located on a part of the city that didn't belong to my brother. I shivered and wrapped my arms around myself when a group of guys walked back and whistled at us. I was ready to leave but I knew that it would hurt Tarma's feelings, so I didn't say a word. A man walked towards us, and I stepped closer to her. She smiled at him, and he smiled at both of us. I wasn't in the mood to be social mainly because he was a stranger.

"Hello ladies, would you like to skip the line and come in with me?"

I opened my mouth to speak but Tarma quickly cut in. She accepted his offer and took his hand when he offered it to her. I looked back at the line and sighed following them to the door. The guy at the door checking IDs didn't pay us much attention. He just waved us in without asking us any questions. They went inside and I followed behind them afraid to lose them. I had never been to a club before, and I didn't know what to do here. The music was loud, and the club was packed with people. There were lights flashing through the room and people on the dance floor. I felt Tarma grab my hand and I squeezed her hand tightly. She giggled and pulled me close reassuring me that I didn't need to be scared. That was easier said than done when you were in an unfamiliar place. We walked over to the bar, and I sat down quickly. My feet were starting to hurt already, I wasn't used to heels. The guy who helped us skip the line handed us each a shot glass. I pushed it away and Tarma instantly looked at me. I mouthed the word no to her and she shrugged gulping hers down.

"Sorry I didn't get to introduce myself properly. My name is Ace, and it is a pleasure to meet you."

"I'm Tarma," she shook his hand and then he turned to me.

"I'm Athena," I smiled weakly shaking his hand.

He laughed, "okay and how old are you two ladies?"

"We are nineteen," Tarma smirked eyeing him up and down.

Ace was very cute. He was tall and very well built. His body was covered in tattoos, which was sexy. He didn't have any facial hair at all. But his blue eyes were something that caught my attention right away. He smiled at me when he saw me staring and I cleared my throat looking away from him.

"Would you like to dance?" He looked at Tarma and she nodded her head quickly.

I grabbed her arm as she hopped down from her seat. She promised me that she wouldn't leave me. The last thing I needed was to be alone in this club. Ace was cute but I couldn't trust him.

 She turned around and giggled, "don't be a baby Athena. I'll be right here."

I watched as she walked to the dance floor with him. I hoped that she had fun tonight so that she wouldn't ever want to do this again. I laughed watching as she danced on him. She definitely needed more practice. There was no doubt that she would be our downfall for getting to the next round. She looked at me and smirked moving closer to him. I knew that she was being a tease, but I didn't want her teasing him too much. Tarma was much wilder, than me and she had lost her virginity at fifteen. I never had the courage to do it because I was afraid. I didn't want to be left heartbroken after the guy got what he wanted. So yes, I was saving myself for marriage. My phone buzzed and I looked down to check and see who was texting me. I smiled looking down at the good night text from my brother.

10:21

R

Roman >

Text Message
Today 4:22 PM

What time are you coming home tonight

I was going to stay the night with tarma. Is that cool???

Why

Because I need girl time 💀 pleaseeeee we will be at her house

I guess but don't leave her house

I won't. Thank you! Love you 🤍

Today 10:20 PM

Good night

Text Message

He was always so sweet when he wanted to be. I shook my head tucking my phone back in my purse. He would be so angry with me if he knew that I was here. There would be no telling what he would do to me if he found out. I shook my head and looked up to see Tarma and Ace gone. I frowned and stood up from my chair looking around for them.

"What happened to not leaving me?" I mumbled pushing my way through the crowd of dancers to find them.

I sighed in relief when I saw her sitting in his lap across the room. I walked over there quickly before I lost her again. Her back was to me, and she looked as though she was making out with him. I rolled my eyes and placed my hand on her shoulder.

"Hey, what happened to not leaving me?"

She turned around slowly, and I stepped back. This woman was not Tarma and the man staring at me was not Ace.

Vain

I stared at the man in front of me. He was
beyond sexy; he was fucking gorgeous.
Everything about him screamed danger but it
was as if he was pulling me in. He sat there and
stared at me, his steel-grey eyes searching my
face for something. He stood up slowly and I
stepped back quickly. He was about the same
height as my brother, if not taller. He had broad
shoulders and muscular arms that were covered
in tattoos. He was covered in tattoos just like
Ace. He left no skin untouched even his face. I
bit my lip and stared at his face once again after
looking over his body. His long eyelashes
kissed his cheeks every time he blinked. He had
high cheekbones and a jaw that could cut

14

through steel and full pink lips that he licked slowly. His dark brown hair was neat and gelled back. It was sleek and precise as if he spent hours in the mirror. I gulped and cleared my throat when he tapped his foot impatiently. Overall, he looked like an asshole, and he was proving that now.

"I-I'm sorry…I didn't mean…I thought that you were someone else." I turned to leave but he stopped me.

"What is your name?"

My knees buckled at how sexy he sounded. His voice was deep and velvet-like. He couldn't hide his heavy Spanish accent if he wanted to.

"I'm Athena," I whispered. He told the girl he was kissing to leave. She walked past me and bumped my shoulder aggressively. I wanted to turn around and tell her off, but I decided against it.

He smirked, "come with me."

I smiled, "no thank you. I'm looking for someone and I really need to get going." I turned to leave once again but he grabbed my hand. I wanted to put up a fight, but I knew that it would end badly for me. I bit my lip allowing him to pull me towards the stairs. I looked back down at the clubbers to see if I could spot Tarma, but she was nowhere to be seen. I rolled my eyes and continued to let him pull me up the stairs. We came to the second floor, and I stared around in amazement. This place was bigger than it looked on the outside. He didn't say a word as we walked to an office down the hall. My heart was pounding in my chest because I was afraid of what he would do. I didn't know him, and he didn't know me. He opened the door and I stepped inside quickly. He smirked and shut the door behind us locking it. He thought that I didn't notice but I did. He still didn't utter a word to me as he made his way over to the bar. I stood in the doorway playing with my hands. I was nervous to be alone with him and he could tell.

"Are you going to just stand there?"

"Oh um…I'm sorry," I whispered walking over to the bar. I took a seat and he smiled gulping down his drink. He pushed a shot glass towards me, and I shook my head quickly. I didn't care for drinking or drugs of any kind. I hated not feeling like myself and I felt like alcohol and drugs clouded your judgment.

He chuckled, "you don't like to drink?"

I smiled weakly, "no. I try to stay away from stuff like that."

He laughed and I clenched my thighs together to try to hide my arousal. His laugh was like music to my ears and his smile made me melt. I had never felt this way before and I found it odd that he had this effect on me. I'm pretty sure he had this effect on a lot of women though.

"You told Ace that you were nineteen and I know you are lying."

My heart stopped in my chest, "how would you know?"

"Because Ace is my right-hand man, and you are Athena Vintalli. You don't think that I wouldn't recognize you?"

I stared at him in shock, "how do you know me? I don't understand because we have never met before."

He smirked, "everyone knows that Roman has a seventeen-year-old sister. I know everything about him because he is my enemy."

I gulped, he couldn't possibly be Vain Grey, could he? I mentally slapped myself, of course, he was. The club was called Grey. I had never seen him before, but I heard a lot about him. He was a man to be feared and I could see why now that I was face to face with him. This was his club, and I was in his territory. I bit my lip and stared at him watching his every move.

"I'm guessing that you know who I am then?"

I nodded my head slowly, "I'll just go. I didn't mean to trespass. I'm sorry," I whispered standing up.

"Tsk tsk...if you think you'll be leaving so soon you're mistaken. Why not have fun with you while I can."

I backed away from him as he came closer. My back hit the wall and I jumped watching him cage me in like an animal. He pulled my body to him, and I whimpered as his grip tightened around my waist. My heart thumped aggressively against my chest waiting for him to make his next move.

"You can't get through life lying…do you know that?" I gasped closing my eyes tight as his words lingered seductively in my ear. A low moan came from his throat as he glided his nose along my cheek and down to my neck. "I asked you a question, love."

"I wasn't the one who lied," I whispered pushing against his chest.

He chuckled, "what beautiful curves you have. Tiny waist, nice perky breasts," he grabbed my ass and squeezed it and I bit my lip harshly. "You're simply perfect," he groaned. Unexpectedly he smashed his lips to mine stealing away my first kiss. I tried to keep up, but he dominated me quickly. He groaned shoving his tongue deeper into my mouth. I could only pull him close to me never wanting him to stop.

He broke away from me quickly and picked me up. I clung to him for dear life trying not to fall.

I couldn't process what was happening because it was all happening so fast. He sat me down on the desk and attacked my neck with open mouth kisses. My eyes rolled back, and I moaned loudly. No man had ever made me feel like this. I had never allowed a man to touch me like this but with him it was different. He didn't stop his assault on my body and that scared me. He slid his hands up my dress and I moaned when his fingers touched my core.

"Vain please."

He chuckled pulling my dress up quickly.

Before I could protest any further, he slid my thong to the side and buried his face in-between my legs. It seemed like I couldn't think straight anymore. I was a moaning mess, and I could tell that he was enjoying it as well. His lips made contact with my sex, and I squirmed around a little bit. His tongue flicked against my clit and I gripped the desk tightly. I moaned his name again as his tongue thrashed, stroked, and sucked.

"You taste delightful," he groaned against my skin.

He held my hips to stop me from squirming as his tongue went deeper. His lips closed over my bud once again and I grabbed the back of his head pushing him deeper. Wet, squelching sounds filled the room and my cries echoed off the walls. My body tightened and I screamed when waves of pleasure hit me. My body bucked and I trembled, throwing my head back. He didn't stop he continued and that prolonged my orgasm.

"Vain...please," I moaned.

I had never experienced an orgasm before, so this was my first time. He smirked and pulled away licking his lips slowly. I stared at him trying to compose myself and catch my breath, but he had other plans. I could hear his belt coming undone and my eyes widened. He pulled his member out and I stared at it in shock, there was no way that he would fit inside me. He spread my legs again and I pushed against his chest.

"No, please...I don't think...we shouldn't." I gulped fixing my clothes.

He growled and grabbed my wrist roughly,

"why are you stopping me?"

"Because I'm not ready," I tried to pry my wrist free from his deathly grip.

He frowned tilting his head to the side, "are you still a virgin?"

Tears came to my eyes as I slowly nodded my head. I knew what he was expecting when he brought me here, but I couldn't give that to him. He was sexy but there was no way that he would love me. He would take my virginity and that would be all there was to it. He would probably act as though I didn't exist. He had endless women at his feet, he didn't need me.

"I'm sorry, I didn't mean to give you the wrong impression. I wasn't coming here to sleep with you," I wrapped my arm around myself.

He ran his fingers through his hair, "you don't look like a virgin. You look like a."

"Don't say that I look like a slut." I interrupted him quickly.

He licked his lips slowly, "you better get going. I don't think that your brother would appreciate you being here."

I nodded my head and ran towards the door. I turned to look at him one more time before pulling the door open and running out. What the hell just happened? Why did I let him do that to me? I shook my head and continued to talk towards the stairs. I needed to get out of here as soon as possible. I walked down the stairs and smiled at Tarma when she ran up to me. She looked a mess; I could tell that she had just had sex.

"Where did you go?"

I shook my head, "it doesn't matter. Can we please leave?"

She grabbed my hand and stared at me. "Did someone hurt you?"

I shook my head quickly, "no. I'm fine I'm just getting tired."

She pulled her phone out of her pocket, "yea. Let's get going because it is two in the morning."

She grabbed my hand and I stared back up at

the top of the stairs. To my surprise there he was, standing there staring down at me. I bit my lip and turned away following Tarma out of the club. I would never see him again so why did it bother me? I was nervous because I just allowed a man to please me. Not only that, I allowed my brother's enemy to do it. What if Roman found out? Would he be angry with me? Should I tell Tarma or no? It was so many questions swirling around in my head. I shook my head and sighed. I wouldn't utter a single word to anyone about this. The fewer people who know the better off I would be. I would just pretend that this night didn't happen. I placed my finger on my lip and closed my eyes, how would I pretend that it didn't happen when I can still feel his hands on me? The images of his face between my legs were turning me on once again. He was good at what he did, but I knew it was because he had been with many women. I had to get him out of my head, the sooner the better.

"Athena, are you sure you're okay?"

I glanced at Tarma, "I will be fine."

She stopped walking and grabbed my hand,

"what happened?"

"Nothing...nothing that I want to talk about." I shrugged and continued to walk with her following closely behind me. I knew that she would continue to question me, but I didn't want to talk about it. I was embarrassed because he was my brother's enemy. I was scared of what he would think if word got out about that. I just hoped that Vain wouldn't say anything.

Amore

One week later

The week passed by in a blur and my brother didn't suspect anything. I was glad that I was able to forget about Vain and that night at the club. I rolled my eyes; I didn't really forget it. For the past few nights, I have been dreaming of him. I have even touched myself thinking about him. What the hell was wrong with me? I mean did I have no dignity left in my body? Touching myself was so embarrassing and I hated it after I found my orgasm. But I couldn't deny that he made me feel things that I had never felt, and my body craved more. I looked up and smiled when I saw the for-sale sign still posted in front of the old building not far from my house. I really wanted this place, but fifteen thousand dollars was not something that I could come up with. My brother wouldn't give me the money no matter how many times I asked him. He just felt like it was pointless to waste money on something I wouldn't be doing in my future. I picked a flower and tucked it in my hair like I did every morning. I stopped by the old building and peeked inside the window looking around. It was so damn perfect but far out of my reach.

"You like this place I see."

My heart stopped in my chest when I heard his voice. I turned around quickly and stepped back gulping. What was he doing here? Vain smiled at me and licked his lips like he was so good for doing. I leaned against the building for support because he was turning me on again. I shook my head trying to chase away the nasty thoughts that clouded my judgment.

"You going to answer me or not? I mean it is rude to ignore someone…Amore." He whispered stepping closer to me again.

I looked around quickly in fear. What if someone saw us together and told my brother about it? I cleared my throat, "yea I like the place."

He pulled a key out of his pocket, "you want to come inside?"

I frowned watching him unlock the door and push it open. How did he get a key to the place unless he bought it? I walked inside and jumped when I heard the door close behind me. I was afraid of being alone with him again. I looked around the place and smiled, it was perfect.

"It's amazing, I just hate that I can't have it," I whispered turning to face him. "What will you be using it for?"

He looked at me confused, "what do you mean?"

"You bought it so what are you going to use it for?"

He laughed, "I think you are mistaken. I didn't buy this; I'm the owner and I'm selling it."

"What?" I whispered. He was the owner? What a small world that we lived in. I laughed and shook my head, "of course you do."

"Let's talk business," he smirked.

I shrugged, "I don't have fifteen thousand dollars. I love the place trust me, but I can't afford it."

He raised an eyebrow, "so your brother won't buy it for you?"

'No, he thinks that dancing is pointless. My future is not with dance, my future is with the mafia. That's what he always says anyway."

"A beautiful woman like you should not be

running a dangerous group. You should be at home making babies. Don't you think?" He whispered walking towards me.

I stepped back as he came closer. I knew where this was going, and I didn't want it to happen again. He grabbed my wrist and pulled me towards him, and I trembled in his arms. I cleared my throat once more and pushed him away.

"Listen, I can't do this with you. I'm seventeen and you're seven years older than me. Besides that, my brother would kill me if he found out."

"So, your brother doesn't know that I pleasured you a week ago? He doesn't know that you were screaming my name?"

"No, and please don't tell him. I can't handle what he would do. I know that he would be upset, and I lied to him that night. Please, don't tell him." I bit my lip feeling his breath on my neck.

He pulled away and stared into my eyes, "I

won't tell him. You don't have to worry about that at all, Amore." I moaned softly feeling his hands slide up my skirt. Here I was again giving in to his touch and lustful words. "This skirt is too short," he groaned rubbing himself against my thigh.

I tried to step aside but he stopped me. I needed to leave because I knew that things would get out of hand. The only problem was I didn't want to leave because my body was begging me to stay. I wanted him to touch me, but I wouldn't admit that to him. Once he got what he wanted he would toss me aside and I refused to be used.

"Why do you act like you don't like my touch? Why do you deny me the one thing I desire?" He whispered squeezing my breast roughly.

'I don't know what you desire," I moaned softly.

"You," he whispered getting down on his knees.

I bit my lip and stared down at him as he hooked my leg over his shoulder. My body was on fire, and I could feel my panties slowly become damp. I wanted him to touch me…I needed him to. He looked up at me and smiled sliding my panties to the side.

"You're so wet for me already."

I gasped and threw my head back when his mouth connected to my throbbing bud. He was so good at what he did, and I needed it. I could hear him slurping at my juices and teasing me slowly with his tongue and it was driving me crazy. I wanted more but I knew that I couldn't. I wasn't ready for more, but I couldn't deny my body either. I screamed feeling my body began to tremble as his tongue slipped inside me. I was so close, and I knew that he could tell because he picked up his pace.

"VAIN…OH MY…YES," I screamed allowing my orgasm to hit me like a wave.

"Mm, I love when you scream my name." He

let me go and I quickly tried to compose myself. I pulled my skirt down and looked down at my feet. Here I was again feeling guilty and dirty after the damage was done.

"I have to get going," I whispered out of breath.

He chuckled, "you have been thinking about me. No matter what you say I know that you pleasure yourself at night to me."

I looked up at him in shock, how did he know that? "I don't know what you mean?"

"Don't play dumb with me. When I first pleasured you, your moans were uncontrollable. You squirmed a lot when I was devouring you. But now, it's like you have gotten used to the feeling. You know what feels good and what spot to touch to set your whole body on fire."

I looked down at my feet, "so what? It's not like it will go any further than this, right? I'm not giving you my virginity so you might as well give up."

He grabbed my chin forcing me to look at him, "I never give up. That's one thing that you will soon realize about me. I always get what I want and what I want is you. So, let's talk business."

I folded my arms across my chest, "what is there to talk about?"

"You want this place and I want you. So, how about this, you dance for me at my club. I'll give you this place for free."

"What do you mean dance for you? Do you want me to dance at club Grey?" I was confused, what type of dancing did he want me to do?

He shook his head, "no. You will be dancing in my private gentleman's club. The type of dancing that you will be doing is not like the dance you do."

I frowned, "so you want me to be a stripper?"

"Yes, that is exactly what I want."

"You're crazy…I would never become a whore

just because I want something. I don't strip, so no thanks." I tried to walk past him, and he grabbed my arm.

"Someone is willing to buy this place in two days. Are you sure that you want to give it up? You will only have to dance on Saturday's and it's only for six months."

I turned around to face him, "I'm seventeen. I can't work at a strip club and besides, I'm not selling myself for this."

He placed his hand on his chin, "don't look at it like you're selling yourself. Look, you don't have to touch anyone...just dance."

"It's not my type of dancing. Don't you understand that I don't want to be a whore?"

"I'll pay you," he interrupted me quickly.

"What?"

He shrugged, "if you don't want to sell yourself than do it for money. You can work for it. I'll give you the key today and then you come by

my place so we can sign the contract. I'll pay
you good money, so it won't seem like you got
it for free. How does this sound, I'll pay you
two thousand dollars every Saturday? I'll take
five hundred and seventy dollars from your
check leaving you with fourteen hundred to
spend how you want. You dance for me for six
months and I'll be paid off."

It was tempting, so tempting. I wanted the
money because my brother never gave me
money. I would be able to save and finally start
getting things for myself. The idea didn't seem
that bad when he was paying me that much
money.

"I don't have to do anything private with
anyone?" I stared at him waiting for him to
answer. I wanted to make sure that he wouldn't
change his mind. The last thing that I wanted
was to become a whore. I didn't mind dancing,
but I didn't want to be doing private shows or
going in the back with men. I had never been to
a strip club, but I heard my brother's friends

talking about it. I would hear them talk about how they took women to the back and what they did with them. It disgusted me and I always promised myself that that would never be me.

"You will only be dancing to entertain. You belong to me so the only person getting a private show is me," he laughed.

"Fine, I will do it."

He smiled, "Good. I'll have my driver pick you up after school."

"I have dance practice so you can pick me up at six. I will be at Bayside Park," I bit my lip.

He grabbed my hand and placed a kiss on it. "I can't wait to see you tonight. We can have dinner at my place and maybe watch a movie."

I rolled my eyes and walked out of the place that I now owned. I was happy because I finally owned the building that I had my eyes on, but I realized that dreams didn't come true.

Everything comes with a price, and this was his price. I looked back and sighed when I saw him watching me. What was the deal with him? Why was he so attached to me? I was way younger than him and he wouldn't be in a serious relationship with me. This was all a game to him, and I was willing to play along. I had six months to be around him, but would I survive? Could I spend six months with him and not give him my virginity?

Contract

I stared out the window watching as the cars
drove by. The red light in front of us was taking
its time turning green. I pulled my phone from
my pocket quickly when I felt it vibrate. My
brother texted me telling me to be careful. I lied
to him again and told him that I was going to go
eat with a few friends. I hated lying to him, but
I wouldn't have to if he just bought the place
for me. The traffic light switched to green, and
the driver took off again. I turned my attention
back out the car window. It was getting dark
fast, and I didn't know how I would get home.

Vain was my brother's enemy so I couldn't have him drop me off at my house. My brother said he was working late tonight but that usually meant that he was messing around with some girl. He rarely brought women to our house but when he did, I knew. The other night he brought a red-haired woman home. She was beautiful but she was nothing but a quick fuck. Roman never cared about any of those women. He took her to his bedroom and had sex with her. I didn't mean to peek, but I was curious, so I cracked the door and watched them for a while. I took a deep breath and closed my eyes. What was happening to me? The car slowed down, and I looked up to see a gorgeous mansion. The house was huge, but I knew that it was because he was a mafia leader. Money was not an issue for them, I mean my house was the same way. I gulped and bit my lip slowly watching as Vain walked out the house. He was expecting me, and he got his wish. The car came to a stop, and he walked up and opened my door. I thanked him softly and climbed out walking towards the house. I heard him say something to the driver, but I couldn't make out what it was. I turned around and he smiled at me, and I rolled my eyes. He was so damn sexy that I hated it.

"Come on in, I won't bite," he chuckled walking behind me.

I didn't respond I just walked into the house. I looked around and smiled. It was very neat and clean for a man to live here alone. He didn't have many pictures on the wall, but he had expensive taste as far as furniture. I tucked a strand of hair behind my ear walking into the living room.

"Can I get you something to drink?"

"Sure, do you have any juice?" I shrugged throwing my bag on the couch.

He laughed, "yea I have juice. You can make yourself at home."

I nodded my head slowly and sat down on the

couch watching him disappear into the kitchen. My heart was pounding in my chest because he made me nervous. He made me so damn nervous that I couldn't control the trembling of my body. I wasn't going to let him see it though. I wouldn't allow him to see that he made me weak because that would be another thing that he could use against me. I looked up when I saw him approaching me carrying a glass. He handed it to me, and I took it thanking him. He sat down beside me and smiled watching me gulp down the Hawaiian punch. I cleared my throat and set the empty glass down on the table.

"How was school?"

I stared at him confused, "um…it was okay. It's school so you can say that it's pretty boring."

He laughed, "do you have a boyfriend?"

"No," I scratched the back of my neck nervously.

He ran his fingers through his hair and sighed,

"so is it just you and your brother?"

"Yea…just me and him. My parents died when I was fifteen in a car accident. So, Roman keeps me close to him. He is very overprotective of me."

He sighed, "I'm sorry to hear about your parents. Your brother has every right to be protective of you. Being in the mafia you have many enemies. Some enemies won't harm a woman or a child. Other mafia leaders don't care."

"I see," I whispered.

"Does your brother allow you to date or is that something you choose?"

I stared into his eyes and bit my lip slowly. Why was he asking so many questions? "My brother doesn't allow me to date. He doesn't want me getting pregnant right now, so boys are off limits."

He laughed, "you're seventeen, right? When

will you be eighteen?"

"June 11th."

"So, you're a Gemini," he smiled grabbing my hand. "Well, my birthday is August 3rd and I'm a Leo. It says that we are compatible."

I frowned laughing, "well what a small world."

He nodded resting his back against the couch and kicking his feet up. We sat in silence for a minute and that made me uncomfortable. I looked up at him watching as he scrolled through his phone. He was so handsome right now. He seemed so relaxed not like the first time that we met. His button up shirt was left open for me to see his tattooed chest and his sweatpants hung loosely on his hips.

"It's rude to stare," he smirked turning to face me.

I looked down at my hands trying to hide my embarrassment. He caught me checking him out. Damn why did I have to stare at him for so long? I mentally slapped myself and sighed wiping my sweaty hands on my skirt.

"What about you? Where are your parents?"

He shrugged, "my father is retired. My mother and father live in Spain."

"Is that where you're from?"

"Yes, I was born in Spain, but the mafia brought me here as a child. My father retired and I took his place when I was eighteen."

"I see," I whispered. "So, why do you and my brother dislike each other?"

"Your brother has the ability to try to overrun me. We split this city in half and yet he is always trying to take over the way I do things. That is my problem with him, but I never really had a conversation with him. I am used to working with your father, so it's new to me."

I stared at him shocked that he mentioned working with my father. I never knew that and Roman never mentioned it to me either. Roman always told me that I wasn't allowed to go to certain parts of the city, and I never knew why. I was young at the time, but I started to ease drop on his conversations and that's when I learned about Vain. "You knew my father? I never knew that."

He nodded his head, "I hated to hear about their deaths. My father and your father were good friends and so it hit my parents hard."

I tilted my head over to the side and sighed. Talking about my parents made me miss them. I still remember hearing about their deaths and being in total shock. They kissed me goodnight and told me that they would see me in the morning. Of course, that never came because they died.

He placed some papers down in front of me and I stared at them. I knew that it was the contract because that was the main reason I was coming here. He handed me a pin and I took it from him. I pulled the papers close to me and was about to sign my name before he stopped me.

"Are you going to read it, love?"

I shook my head and signed my name, "no. We talked about everything already so there is no need to read over it." I handed him the contract and his pin, and he chuckled. What was funny now?

"Has no one ever taught you to read before you agree to things? You really should, my sweet Athena." He opened the contract to the second page, "You agree to come to me every Saturday and give me a private show. I am allowed to touch you wherever I please and you can't stop me."

I frowned and snatched the piece of paper from him. He couldn't have snuck that in there. Why would he do that? I stared up at him and he licked his lips slowly. If he didn't look so damn sexy, I would have slapped him.

"Why would you add that in here? I told you that."

"It doesn't matter what you told me, Athena,"

he interrupted me quickly. "I want you and I will have you besides I already told you that."

I stood up and grabbed my bag, "I'll see you Saturday."
 He grabbed my hand, "I'll be picking you up Saturday. So, you need to tell me a place that is convenient for you."

I snatched my hand away, "I'll let you know."

"Where are you going?" He growled walking up behind me.

"I'm going home. I don't have to see you until Saturday so that is when I will see you."

He chuckled, "you're not going anywhere. It's dark outside and I've already made dinner."

I licked my lips and sighed running my fingers through my hair. "Why are you forcing yourself on me? You have endless women at your feet but yet you pursue me...why?"

He grabbed my hand and pulled me close to him. "You're not like all those other women.

They are nothing but whores that I use for a quick fuck. You're so pure and innocent. If you just give me a chance...I can show you that I want more with you."

I looked at him confused, "you just met me. If I wasn't a virgin than you wouldn't be saying any of this. If I had let you have sex with me that night at the club...you would treat me like you treat all those other women."

He shook his head, "you're wrong."

"How?" I whispered.

He backed me against the wall brushing his lips against mine. I closed my eyes placing my hand on his chest. "I would never hurt you."

I looked away when he tried to capture my lips in a kiss. He growled and grabbed my wrists roughly and I winced in pain. What was his problem?

"Stop being such a stuck-up brat."

I tried to get my hand free, "you're hurting me

let go." He shoved me away from him roughly and cradled my wrist in my hand. He turned his back to me, and I just stood there afraid to move. What was he going to do to me? He became so angry so fast. Standing here I couldn't help but realize that maybe I made the wrong decision signing that contract.

I walked around him and grabbed my bag quickly. I wasn't going to stay here like this. I turned around to leave but he stood there in front of me. I stepped back and he stepped closer until I was trapped between him and the couch.

"I told you that you're not leaving tonight."

"Vain, I don't want to," I whispered.

He cupped my chin, "you signed a contract and now you belong to me. Don't argue with me just do what I said. Now go get cleaned up for dinner."

I took a deep breath and nodded my head slowly. He smiled and kissed my head before walking into the kitchen. I walked down the hallway quickly, my heart was going a mile a minute. I had to get out of here and fast. I opened the bathroom door and stepped inside locking it. I stared at the window and smiled. I didn't waste any time pulling the curtains open and fidgeting with the lock. To my surprise the lock on the window was not an ordinary lock.

"Looking for a way out?"

I gasped and turned around quickly, "I was just."

He shook his head walking towards me slowly. Why are you so disobedient? I see why your brother has to punish you."

"Vain please…"

He raised an eyebrow and stared at me, "I told you that I wouldn't hurt you. So, you don't have to be afraid. I lost my temper back there and I'm sorry. Please just come have dinner with me and let me make it up to you."

He offered me his hand and I took it allowing him to lead me into the kitchen. What was I going to do?

First Day

I pulled the door open and stepped inside before anyone could see. This club was similar to club Grey. It was big on the inside but not on the outside. It was a two-story building just like the other one. Instead of a dance floor, there were chairs and tables. Booths lined the walls and a huge stage covered one half of the room. I took a deep breath and gulped. I had never been to a strip club before, and I was nervous. I didn't even know how to strip or tease a man. Three girls sat at the bar gossiping they pretended not to notice me. As I walked towards them, they stood up and walked away quickly.

"Rude," I mumbled under my breath. Once again, I was alone in the room. I wished that I could be honest with Tarma. Having her here would make this so much easier for me. I sat down at the bar and closed my eyes. Maybe this was a bad idea. Maybe I needed to give him back his key and cancel the deal. I shook my head, I couldn't. I had already shown everyone the studio and they loved it. How could I take it away from them now? As much as I hated this, I had to follow through with it. It was only 6 months, and I was only here on Saturdays so it couldn't be that bad.

"I see you made it."

I turned around quickly when I heard his voice. He looked sexy today, I mean he looked sexy every day. He had on a suit and tie and his hair was gelled back nice and neat as usual. He smiled at me, and I rolled my eyes at him. He chuckled and whistled loudly. After he did that seven girls walked into the room quickly. He smiled at them, and they all greeted him at the same time.

"Listen, ladies, this is our newbie. You can call her...baby doll." He looked at me up and down and smirked, "yes, that will do just fine. Now, each one of you introduce yourself."

A woman with long red hair and blue eyes stepped in front of the group. She had a lollipop in her mouth which she quickly removed to speak. "My name is Candy," she smiled sticking the sucker back in her mouth. She was a little taller than me and her body was way more developed than mine.

"I'm Kitten, it's nice to meet you." The woman who spoke was very pretty. She was about the same height as me. She had shoulder-length black hair and brown eyes. Her voice was gentle, and she seemed a little frightened just like a kitten. She didn't have many curves, but her body was still nice.

The third woman who stepped up was Asian. She had long black hair that touched her waist and brown eyes. She reminded me of Kitten as far as the shape of her body. She was also very pretty even with the tattoos that covered her arms. She also had a tattoo of a lily on her chest. "My name is Lillie," she smiled at me, and I smiled back.

The woman who stepped up next was the woman from earlier. She was the one who told the other girls to get up and leave with her. She had silky blonde hair, green eyes that sparkled, and a nice body. "Roxy." That's all she said before turning her back to me.

"My name is Diamond." I looked at her and she smiled at me. She had beautiful brown skin, brown eyes, and pretty white teeth. Her body was perfect and so was she. Although she was rude to me in the beginning, I could tell she was still a nice person.

A woman with long brown hair with blonde highlights smiled at me. She was petite in size, but her body still had perfect curves. She had brown eyes and had a heavy Spanish accent. "My name is Sunny and I'm Mexican. A lot of people get me confused with Puerto Rican you know."

The last woman to step up was a woman with red hair. It was cut into a bob, and she had blue eyes. When she walked away with Roxy earlier, I noticed a tattoo of a cherry on her butt. She smiled at me, "My name is Cherry and I'm sure you know why."

Vain clapped his hands and smiled, "great. Now that introductions are over, I need someone to show baby doll around. Hmm, how about you Kitten? Do me the honor please and show her around."

Before we could protest, he walked away leaving me alone with the women I just met. Kitten smiled at me and waved for me to follow her. I was still nervous but at least he paired me with someone nice. Roxy was a bitch, and I knew we would not be friends.

Kitten looked over her shoulder at me and smiled. "Just ignore Roxy. She sees any new girl as competition, and she tries to run them away."

"Competition for what exactly?" I wasn't sure what she meant. What could you possibly compete for in a strip club?

"Money, clients, and Vain. She doesn't like the

idea of his eyes being on anyone else. They are kind of like a thing." She rolled her eyes and shrugged.

For some reason hearing that she liked Vain made me angry. I know that it was stupid though. What woman wouldn't like him; I mean look at him. On top of that, Vain was not the type to settle down. He was used to sleeping around but he wasn't going to do it to me.

So, this is the dressing room. Vain picks out your outfits for the first two months. So, you won't have to worry about dressing rules just yet. We walked inside and I looked around in amazement. There were rows of mirrors and chairs. Each one of the women that I met earlier was sitting at one doing their makeup and hair. It looked like a room for a famous person. Kitten walked out and I followed behind her quickly. She stood by the staircase and pointed up. "That is where Vain's office is. There are also rooms up there for special occasions."

I stared at her confused, "what special occasions?"

"Business meetings, mafia-related business, and so on. We don't go up there unless Vain calls us to his office." She turned around and pointed to a dark red curtain hanging in the back of the room. "Back there are several rooms. That is where we take the men who want a little extra. We are not allowed to have sex with them. We can only please them with our hands. We are not whores and this not a whore house...as Vain likes to put it. Just a heads up, men will try it, but you have to stay strong. They even tempt you with money and it can be hard to deny."

"Have any men ever tried to get you to do more?"

She giggled, "of course. I've been here for three years, and I've lost count of how many men ask. This one girl who used to work here made the mistake of accepting a client's offer. Her name was Sparkle and she was gorgeous. Well, the guy offered her five thousand dollars for a night between her legs. She accepted, but when Vain found out it was terrible for her. Word is he makes her work the streets now...you know as a prostitute. He said if she wanted to act like

a whore, he was going to treat her like one."
She shrugged, "moral of the story…don't do it.
I don't care if they offer you a million dollars.
Besides Vain pays us great, we don't need to do
that stuff."

I frowned, "but aren't you still selling yourself
when you touch a man though?" I was
confused. They were still pleasing them so what
made it different? What was the difference
between having sex and jacking them off?

Kitten shook her head, "we aren't selling our
vaginas. We are selling our hands. You can't
get an STD on your hands, now can you?"

I shrugged, "okay so you have a point. But
what about if they want to touch us? What if
they ask us to get naked, do we?"

She smiled, "I'm glad you're asking a lot of
questions. The answer to that is no. We don't
get naked, and they don't touch us. We are here
to give pleasure not to receive. Besides, them
touching you is another way for them to bait
you into fucking. Keep your clothes on at all
times. Hell, dance on them to get them off but

don't let them have sex with you. All of them
know the rules but they will try it anyway. With
you being new they will try you a lot more."

I nodded my head quickly, "okay is there
anything else I need to know?"

She frowned, "When Vain whistles that means
he is calling for a group meeting. Never ignore
the whistle because it pisses him off. Always be
ready by seven o clock because the club opens
at eight. Your shift starts at eight and ends at
two in the morning. You can't drink, that's the
most important part. I can't believe I almost
forgot that," she sighed hitting her head. "You
are not allowed to drink before your shift and
during your shift. You know alcohol sways
your actions. Never accept a drink from any of
the men here. They will spike it, trust me. Other
than that, it's pretty simple. Vain is really easy
going and he cares about us so never be afraid
to be honest with him. Even when it comes to
your monthly cycle, he will make arrangements
for you."

I bit my lip, "got it. Thank you, you were very
helpful." I was nervous about being here. I

knew that if Roman found out I was a dead woman. There was no way in the world that he would ever forgive me. I shook my head; there I went again doubting myself. It was only six months and one day out the week. I could do this no problem.

Kitten grabbed my hand, "come on. We have to get you dressed."

I nodded my head and allowed her to pull me along. This was going to be a long night.

I took a deep breath and stared at myself in the mirror. I didn't look like myself at all. It reminded me of the time that I allowed Tarma to get me dressed up. I closed my eyes and licked my lips slowly. Kitten curled my hair and did my makeup. My eye shadow was a dark blue faded into a light blue. Glitter covered the cut crease that Kitten created. My lips were full and plump and coated with red lipstick. The outfit that vain had chosen for me hugged all my small curves. The outfit was similar to a school uniform, but it showed more and was covered in glitter and rhinestones. The crop top tied in the middle and only covered my breasts. Everything else was on full display for men to see. The skirt was shorter than my school skirt and the only thing covering my vagina was a white thong. The stockings that I wore were thigh high and they were black. Last but not least the heels. There were five-inch blue heals that were open toe and covered with blue rhinestones. Overall, I was covered with glitter and rhinestones. When I saw what the other women were wearing it made me feel better about my outfit. They wore literally nothing.

"Aww baby doll you look so cute," Diamond smiled standing beside me.

I looked her up and down slowly, "you are perfect."

She giggled fixing her bra, "I'm nothing compared to you."

Roxy walked up to Diamond and slapped her

hand away. Diamond cursed at her and smiled as Roxy started fixing her bra for her. "How old are you? Are you even legal to work here, I mean you look like a child?"

Diamond rolled her eyes, "come on Roxy stop being rude to her."

Roxy shrugged, "I'm just asking."

"No, you're just being a bitch." Diamond looked over at me, "do you like Vain? As in do you want to have sex with him." I shook my head quickly and she smiled turning her attention back to Roxy. "There you go. Now you see that she doesn't want your man."

Roxy laughed, "as if she could ever get him."

Vain walked into the room and smiled at us all. His eyes lingered on me a little longer than they should have but I ignored him. "Okay ladies, it's showtime. We have a full house so do your best tonight."

Craving Him

I walked around offering drinks to the men sitting at the tables. The other girls were on stage dancing. It wasn't so bad in here as long as I didn't have to dance. I knew how to dance but not like these women. I didn't know about pole dancing, and I was scared, to be honest. I didn't want to go on stage and be booed off. I would feel embarrassed and that would make me want to give up. Luckily for me, Vain said that I could just serve drinks. It was pretty simple; I go get a tray from the bar and walk around the tables. The men sometimes would wave me off or take a drink off the tray. I walked to a table and a handsome man smiled at me. I politely returned the smile and offered him a drink. He was covered in tattoos just like Vain. I knew just by looking at him that he was a Mafia leader as well. I couldn't tell which group he was from, but it was a big one.

"What's your name?" He smiled winking at me.

"Baby doll…can I get you another drink?" I wanted to get the conversation off of me.

He laughed, "what's your real name?"

This guy was cute but annoying. Why did he want my real name? One thing was for certain, I wasn't going to give it to him. If word got out that a girl named Athena works here my brother would freak. It was going to be best if I kept my identity a secret. I smiled at him and placed his drink down in front of him. "My name is Baby doll. That's the only name that I answer to now."

He sat back in his chair and looked me up and

down slowly. "Well, baby doll you look gorgeous tonight. How about we go to the back?" I froze when I felt his hand travel up my thigh. I kept telling myself to breathe but it wasn't working. This man was about to get slapped in the face if he didn't remove his hand.

"How about you get your hand off me and jack off yourself." I picked up the drink and threw it on his face. He stood up and I backed away quickly. I knew that he was going to be pissed off, but he shouldn't have touched me.

"You stupid little bitch," he roared and reached for me. Before he could get his hands on me Vain stepped in front of me.

"Is there a problem here?"

"Hell yeah, there's a problem. That little girl over there threw a drink on me. What the hell man, is that how you train your strippers?"

Vain looked back at me and I gulped. I could see the anger in his eyes, and I knew I was in trouble. "No, I'm sorry that she did that. She is

new and tonight is her first night. Look, to
make things right I'll give you a week of free
drinks. Trust me when I say that it won't
happen again, Adonis."

I frowned when I heard him say the man's
name. Adonis Patel was the leader of a mafia
group in Chicago. He would travel back and
forth from England to Chicago. He was known
for killing in cold blood. There were rumors
that he made women work the streets for him as
well, but I was unsure. He was the biggest and
the richest mafia leader currently. No one
wanted war with him because of how big his
group was.

Adonis looked at me and smirked, "if you want
to make things right then give me the girl. I
want her for a night and then she can prove how
sorry she is."

Vain sighed, "I can't do that."

He looked at Vain and frowned, "you said that
you would make this right."

Vain laughed, "I said that I would make things right and give you a week of free drinks here. Big brother, you know how I operate. You know that I don't sell my strippers. If I want them to be whores, I give them to you. Besides, this little baby doll is mine."

Adonis chuckled, "I see. Well, now I know that she is off-limits. But make sure when you're done with her, you give her to me. A pretty face like that shouldn't go to waste." He turned around and picked up his jacket. Vain pulled him into a hug and then turned to face me.

"My office now."

I placed the tray down on the table and walked towards the staircase. I knew that he was going to lecture me, but I didn't care. I took the steps one by one because I wanted to give myself more time. I could feel him right behind me and so I picked up the pace. Once I got to the top of the stairs, he pointed to a door that was located on the left. I walked inside quickly, and he followed me slamming the door behind him.

"What the hell was that, huh?" He walked over to his desk and sat down.

"He touched me, and I was just."

"I don't care what you were just doing. He is a client and not any client. He spends twenty thousand dollars here a week. You are here to please all my clients. If they want to touch you, then let them. I gave you an easy job and you are still messing it up."

I sighed, "look I'm sorry."

"You're not sorry," he interrupted me again. He took a deep breath and sat back down in his chair. "Come here."

I was afraid to go over to him. I knew that he was angry, and I didn't want to be punished. He scared me the night I was at his house to sign the contract. His temper is terrible. "Vain please I just want to."

He looked at me slowly, "I said come here."

I gulped and walked towards him slowly. My

legs were trembling, and goosebumps covered my skin. What would he do to me? I knew that he was angry, but would he be angry enough to hurt me? I walked around his desk and he turned to face me. I could see the anger in his eyes but there was something else. I couldn't figure out what it was, but I knew that it couldn't be good.

He grabbed my arm and pulled me towards him. I could only stand there and stare down at my feet. The thoughts of what was coming next ate at me.

"You have been tempting me all night," he closed his eyes and placed his hands on my hips. "You're so sexy, amore." He smiled running his hands down my legs slowly. I could feel myself growing weaker the more he touched me. He sat back in his chair and licked his lips, "dance for me."

I stared at him confused, "what do you mean?"

He chuckled, "I want you to dance on me. I

know that you've been watching the other girls. So, now I want you to practice on me."

Was he crazy? I didn't know how to dance like that. I was only used to hip hop dancing with my dance crew. I knew that I was going to embarrass myself and that wasn't going to happen. I tried to walk away but he grabbed my arm and shook his head. "You're not going anywhere until you dance for me. I will keep you here all night."

"Fine," I mumbled. The sooner I got this out of the way the better. If I danced for him than I could leave and go back downstairs. I didn't want to be alone with him and he knew that. It was as if he enjoyed making me feel uncomfortable. He tapped his foot impatiently which broke me out my trance. I turned around and I slowly moved my hips. I wasn't sure what I was doing but it felt right so I kept going. I felt his hands on my waist and I gasped as he pulled me closer to his lap.

"You have to get closer," he whispered in my

ear.

I took a deep breath and closed my eyes. I kept swaying my hips from side to side slowly. I could feel him growing in his pants and that's when I knew I was turning him on. He placed his hands on my hips and helped guide me up and down as I danced on him. It was as if I was making love to him with my clothes on. I could hear him groan in my ear as he grabbed a fist full of my hair.

"You are mine," he groaned placing sloppy kisses on my neck.

I could only moan in response as things took a fast turn. One minute I was dancing on him to get it over with. The next minute I was enjoying what he was doing to me. He slammed me down on his lap and parted my legs quickly. I wanted to protest but he placed his mouth against mine. I closed my eyes trying to match the speed of his tongue, but he dominated me. I could feel his hands all over my body and I didn't want to stop it. He grabbed my right

breast and squeezed it roughly and when I
gasped, he broke the kiss. I could only say his
name before a loud moan escaped my lips. His
fingers had found their way into my thong and
were now attacking my sensitive bud. All I
could do was moan and claw at his shirt as he
brought me closer to my peak. I was so close
that my body started to tremble uncontrollably.
Right when I was about to find my release, he
pulled his fingers away. I stared at him, and he
smiled at me licking his lips slowly.

"Are you okay baby doll, you look a little
flustered?"

I frowned trying to catch my breath. Damn, he
was playing with me again. I stood up and fixed
my clothes quickly. This was getting more and
more out of hand. How much further would I
let him go? I took a deep breath and turned
around to leave but he stopped me.

"I wasn't finished with you yet. Next time you
upset one of my clients you won't be brought
here for pleasure. I robbed you of an orgasm

because you didn't deserve it."

I shook my head and turned to face him, "Is that what you do with the other women when they misbehave?"

He chuckled, "someone's jealous I see."

"I'm not jealous. I just want you to stop trying to have sex with me. I'm not stupid and I know that you and Roxy mess around. So instead of pleasuring me, you need to call her in here tonight so she can get you off."

He shook his head, "you can think what you want. I don't care but I don't deal with Roxy."

"I'm sure you don't. If you don't mind, I'll be getting back to work. The sooner I pay you off the better." I walked towards the door but when I heard him stand up, I stopped. What did he want now? I turned around to confront him, but I was slammed against the wall. I gasped feeling him lift me into his arms with ease. My lips were just inches away from his and my legs were around his waist. I could feel him pressing himself against my core and it was driving me crazy.

"I'm starting to think that you enjoy pissing me off. Let me tell you something...I will drive you insane. I can make you crave me in the worst ways. And there will be nothing you can do about it. I can make you feel things you've never felt, Athena. Your body is my playground and when I start playing, I don't stop. I suggest you stop testing me because I'm running out of patience with you. Next time you disrespect me I won't hesitate to make you crave me. Trust me," he whispered brushing his lips against mine.

He let me go and opened the door leaving the room quickly. I could only stand there trying to stop my heart from racing. He had me craving him already and I didn't want another taste of that. I walked over to the couch and sat down. I needed a moment before I returned to work.

The Fair

I groaned and rolled over shielding my eyes from the sun. I got home at three this morning and I passed out. I was exhausted and my feet were killing me. I grabbed my pillow and put it over my face. The sun disappeared and I smiled snuggling deeper under the covers. Today was Sunday and I had dance practice, but I was being lazy. I didn't want to go because I was sore from work last night. I sighed; I didn't see Vain before I left. He had one of his drivers take me home instead of him. It wasn't a good idea for him to bring me home anyway. I didn't want him knowing where I lived. At the end of the day, he was still Roman's enemy, and I was betraying my brother. Not only that, but I was also betraying his trust. He trusted me and I was lying to him. I felt bad about it because he only wanted what was best for me.

"ATHENA!"

I pushed the pillow off my face and sat up quickly when I heard my brother yell my name. His screaming this early in the morning couldn't be good. Had he found out about me being around Vain? My room door swung open, and he walked in holding my bookbag.

"What did I tell you about leaving your bookbag in the middle of the floor?"

I closed my eyes and thanked god silently. I thought that he had found out about me creeping around. I placed my hand on my heart and shook my head. I felt like a huge weight was lifted off my shoulders.

"Well, are you going to explain yourself or not?"

I looked at him and scratched my head nervously, "I'm sorry. I know that you said to never do it and I don't know why I forgot. It won't happen again, I promise."

He rolled his eyes, "you said that last time." He turned his back to me and dropped my bookbag by my door.

In a strange way, I wanted him to stay. We didn't get to spend much time together and I missed my brother. It seemed like every time we spoke to each other we were arguing about something. We got along when mom and dad were alive but once they died, he drifted away. "Roman, I was wondering if we could do something today. You know just you and me?"

"I can't, I'm busy today. I thought that you had something to do with your friends anyway."

I shrugged, "I can always cancel. I just want to spend a day with you. It doesn't have to be the whole day."

He turned towards me and smirked, "what do you have in mind?"

I placed my hand on my chin and frowned, "hmm…how about we go to the fair. You know the fair just opened the other day for the spring fling."

He sighed, "if you want to go then we will go."

I smiled, "Good. I'll be ready in an hour. Please try to smile today. You always look so grumpy."

He rolled his eyes, "you're already getting my precious time. Now you want me to smile …yea…no."

I laughed and picked up my pillow tossing it at him. Before I could hit him, he ran out of the room and slammed the door. I needed this more than ever. Just a day to relax and have fun with my brother. I climbed out of bed and smiled; it was time to get dressed. I walked to my closet and pulled out a blue jean jacket, white jeans, and a white spaghetti strap t-shirt. I grabbed my black and white tennis shoes and walked towards the bathroom to shower.

I held my stomach and laughed grabbing Roman's hand. He always hated the Farris wheel, but I loved it. He shook his head and pulled me into a tight hug. I was shocked at first but quickly hugged him back.

"I'm glad that we are spending time together. I do miss you a lot, but I know that you're busy." I pressed my head against his chest, and he laid his cheek on my head.

"I know, I miss you too Athena. By the way, we are never doing that again." We both looked up at the Farris wheel and laughed. I would be lying if I said that hearing him laugh brought me joy. I missed seeing him happy like this. It seemed like being the leader of the mafia made him bitter and angry. I hated seeing him like that because I know that he deserves to be happy. I would have to start bringing him out more if that means making him smile. Maybe that would bring back some of the happiness that he lost.

"You hungry?"

I nodded my head quickly, "I'm starving."

He laughed, "I thought so. Come on, let's get some food."

We walked over to the hotdog stand and Roman got two Chicago style hotdogs and loaded fries. He got a lemonade for me and strawberry lemonade for him. He handed the man twenty dollars and told him to keep the change. As we waited for our food we stood there in silence. Great, now we were back to being silent.

"Is there anything you want to talk to me about?"

I looked at him surprised. Now we were doing small talks about life. I smiled and tucked a strand of hair behind my ear. "Um…not that I know of. What about you?"

He shook his head and shrugged, "not really. I mean I haven't really checked on you. How is school and your grades? Are you doing well?"

The man handed us our food and I smiled thanking him. Roman walked over to a nearby staircase and we took a seat. I didn't waste any

time biting into my hotdog. I closed my eyes
and savored the taste of the peppers and onions.
The Chicago hotdog is my favorite and I order
it anytime I go to a hotdog cart.

I cleared my throat and swallowed my food,
"school is fine. I'm acing all my classes, so you
don't have to worry about my grades."

He nodded his head, "okay so what about boys?
Any boys in your life?" He lifted his hotdog to
his mouth and took a bite waiting for me to
answer.

I raised an eyebrow at him, "are we really going
to talk about boys?"

"Yea," he said with a mouth full of food. I
laughed and grabbed a napkin wiping the
ketchup off the side of his mouth. "I want you
to be honest with me about anything. Especially
boys because you are at the time in your life
where you get interested."

I smiled taking a sip of my lemonade, "I
thought you said that I couldn't have a
boyfriend."

"You can't," he said taking another bite of his hotdog. "Look, I don't want it to seem like I'm controlling you. I just don't want you to be like all these other girls. I mean look at Tarma. I know that she is far from innocent."

I took a deep breath and placed my hand on his shoulder. "I won't end up like them because I know what I want. I know that boys say anything to get me in bed and I'm not going for it."

He looked at me smiled, "you can date when you're thirty."

I rolled my eyes, "you sound like dad."

He laughed, "I just want to keep you safe. I know that I can't stop you from falling in love. You will have to learn for yourself one day, but I don't want you to make a mistake. I don't want you to get pregnant right now. You have your whole life ahead of you Athena."

I stuffed some of my fries in my mouth, "I won't."

He shook his head and grabbed a napkin wiping away some cheese on the side of my face. "I want you to come to me when you think you might take the next step. I know this is probably something that mom would tell you but she's not here. I just want to make sure that you're safe while doing it at least."

I bit my lip, "you don't have to worry. I'm not interested right now. Sex is the last thing on my mind. I mean graduation is three months away. I'm just trying to prepare for that."

"Good," he mumbled digging into his fries.

I loved my brother, and I knew that I should be honest with him. But he would be angry and confront Vain. And then the truth would come out about everything that I've done so far. Roman would be so angry that he would never let me leave the house again. Maybe if I paid off Vain then I wouldn't have to work for him. If I could just talk Roman into giving me fifteen thousand dollars, then I wouldn't have to lie anymore.

I licked my lips and watched him eat. My heart was pounding in my chest, but I knew I had to at least ask. "Roman, I was wondering if you could give me fifteen thousand dollars."

"Is it for that dance studio thing? Look, we already talked about that. You need to stop wasting your time dancing and start preparing to deal with Mafia business."

I interrupted him before he could go any further with his lecture. "I know, but dancing is the only thing that makes me focus. I don't focus on boys because dancing keeps me busy. My grades are perfect. I wouldn't ask if it wasn't important to me. Please Roman, this would mean the world to me. I'll even start learning about the Mafia bank accounts. I know that I will have to keep the money safe and accounted for." I was willing to do anything to pay off Vain so that I wouldn't have to see him anymore.

He looked at me and sighed, "I'll think about."

"You promise?" I placed my hand on his shoulder.

"Yea, I promise." He smiled weakly.

I stared up at the sky and smiled. There was finally a chance that I would be able to pay off Vain. I would never have to see him again and everything would be perfect. I took another bite of my fries and watched as a group of birds flew towards the sun. It was such a beautiful day, and I didn't want it to end but I knew Roman was a busy man. He stood up and dusted himself off before turning his attention to me.

"You want to ride a few more rides?"

I nodded my head quickly and stood up. I grabbed his hand and tossed our empty food containers in the garbage can nearby. Roman didn't hesitate to pull me towards the knockout ride. Just looking at it I knew I was going to be sick. We walked over to the line, and I leaned against my brother just to be close to him. I heard a woman laughing and I looked over to see a gorgeous woman with blonde hair. She slapped a man on the arm and the smile melted from my face when I saw that it was Vain. He handed her a teddy bear and she squealed with excitement. My heart stopped in my chest when she pressed her lips against his. He didn't deny her kiss, he welcomed it. I shook my head and looked away. Why the hell did I care anyway? I mean it's not like he was my boyfriend or anything like that. He was a man who got around, and I knew that. That's why I couldn't get attached to him. I knew that was easier said than done but I wouldn't have to deal with him much longer anyway. Roman was going to give me the money so I was going to pay him off. I looked over once again and he was staring at me. I pretended not to notice him and turned back towards my brother to start a conversation.

Regret

I stared at myself in the mirror as I danced. I finally got the dance studio set up and it was perfect. I missed dancing and I couldn't help but realize that I've been slacking. I sighed and grabbed the radio remote and switched off the radio. BoA, eat you up was the name of the song we were supposed to be dancing too. I loved the song, and she was my idol, but I couldn't focus. Everyone had left an hour ago, but I was still here practicing. I ran my hands through my hair and stared at my reflection. My white crop top and grey sweatpants matched the idea for the song. But for some reason I was struggling with getting the steps right. I shook my head and started to do the steps again without the music.

"When I first saw you, I knew nothing's like it used to be." I sang to myself. I kicked my foot out and then popped my chest to match the beat in my head. I smiled and kept singing, "I'll eat you up, your love your love."

I heard someone clapping and I stopped and turned around to see Vain leaning against the wall. I placed my hand on my hip and licked my lips. What the hell was he doing here? I hadn't seen him in three days. I didn't want to see him until Saturday, and I really didn't want to see him then. I was trying to avoid him as much as I could, but the feeling wasn't mutual. He wanted to be around me as much as he could.

"That's impressive, Amore."

"What are you doing here?" I frowned.

"I was in the area, and I decided to stop by and see how you were doing. I was starting to miss you and I knew I could find you here." He smiled walking towards me.

I stepped back, "I would like to make this about business. We shouldn't be seeing each other when I'm not at work."

He smirked, "what would be the fun in that?"

"Vain, I told you before that I don't want to be with you. If you're looking to sleep with me, it's not going to happen. Besides, my brother is going to give me the money to pay you off."

He chuckled, "really? I guess you were discussing that with him when you were at the fair with him?"

"Yes, I did. I'm not trying to get on his bad side." I walked towards the door and grabbed my bag.

"So, you pay me off and then what? Do you think that's going to make me stop seeing you?

Don't be stupid, Athena. What I want I always get."

I balled my hands into fists and turned towards him. "Why do you want me anyway? You have endless women at your feet but yet you want me. Why? What do I have that those women aren't giving you? You're full of crap and you know it. Just leave me alone Vain."

He walked towards me and grabbed my arm pulling me against his body. I struggled against him, but he pinned me to the wall. "Stop denying that you want it too. The only reason that you're trying to get away from me is so that you don't fall in love with me. You know you love the things I do to you. You know that you are addicted to me, and you want more from me."

"Let go of me Vain," I tried to punch his chest, but he blocked my attacks.

"Be honest with yourself. The only reason that you won't give me a chance is because of your brother. If you didn't like me then you would have never let me pleasure you twice. You enjoy my touch, and you know that you do. Just be honest with me…tell me how you really feel."

I took a deep breath staring into his eyes. "I find you attractive and I may have developed a crush on you. But we are seven years apart we can't be together. You are my brother's enemy, and I can't choose you over my family. We will never be able to be more, and you know that." It was true I mean I liked Vain. I did crave his touch and although I tried to make it seem like I hated his presence I liked it deep down. I just couldn't keep up with the life he was living, and I wasn't about to get my heartbroken.

He sighed, "how do you know what we can be if you don't try?"

I shook my head, "there's no need to try. I saw you at the fair with that girl. Why don't you go and be with her?"

"Because I don't want her. I want you," he whispered brushing his lips against my cheek.

"For now, next week you'll be on to the next best-looking thing."

He smirked, "what if I can prove that I can be with only you. Would you be with me then?"

I rolled my eyes at him, "as if you could do that."

"I can and I will."

I placed my hand on his chest and pushed him away. "Well, actions speak louder than words. I have to get going because it's getting late." I tried to walk past him, but he stepped in front of me. I tried to protest but he picked me up and wrapped my legs around his waist. I could feel his lips on my neck, and I could only bite my bottom lip to silence my moan. He walked into the room that I used as my office and sat me down on the desk.

He parted my legs and stood between them so

that he could still access my neck. I arched my
back and moaned softly. As much as I tried to
hide it, he still was able to hear it. "Let me
show you how I can make you feel. Let me
worship your body like you deserve."

"Vain…please," I whispered. "I can't do this."

He ignored me and grabbed my sweatpants
pulling them down to my ankles along with my
panties. He grabbed my shoes and yanked them
off my feet before yanking my pants off my
body completely. He brought his lips back up to
my neck and started to attack it once more.
Once again, he was drawing me in, and I
couldn't fight it. A part of me wanted to and I
needed that part to help me right now. I bit my
lip and once again gathered up the courage to
tell him to stop.

"You don't want this?" He whispered.

"Vain."

He pressed his lips against mine and I kissed
him back instantly. What was he doing to me? I

knew what he was about but yet I couldn't gather up enough strength to stop him. I couldn't deny him and that's because I wanted it too. I had never been touched like this before and I craved it.

"Athena, let me give you pleasure. Tonight, I want you to let go. For once don't fight me, just let it happen."

How could I let it happen when I felt so guilty afterward? I felt dirty just doing this with him. I had never shown any man my vagina but yet he saw it. I felt like I was going too far with him, and it wasn't a good thing. Before I could utter a single word, he spread my legs and kneeled down in front of me. Without giving any thought to what he was doing he slowly dragged his tongue against my clit and kissed it. When he pulled away, I whimpered with need. I wanted him to bring me to a release. I was addicted to the feeling and now I wanted it more and more. He smirked and thrust his tongue between my folds. My loud moan not only shocked him, but it shocked me as well. I gripped the edge of the desk when I felt his tongue slide inside me. I wanted more but I was afraid to ask. I knew that by asking I was feeding into his desire for me. But I couldn't help it, I couldn't hold it in anymore.

"Please," I whispered. "Please…I want more. Vain please."

He groaned and quickly started to devour me. The sound of him sucking at my flesh and drinking my juices brought me to my orgasm. My eyes rolled back, and I screamed his name as my body shook uncontrollably. I moaned his name over and over again until my body finally relaxed from the tiny sparks that shot threw me. He stood up and I could see the lust in his eyes. I couldn't stop my body from trembling, and I felt weak. I watched him unbutton his shirt and my eyes trailed down his tattooed chest. He was so sexy, and I wanted him. I shook my head trying to come back to my senses. I looked at him and watched as he undid his belt. He unbuttoned his pants and slid them down and his erection sprang free. I placed my hand on his chest to stop him as he came closer. I didn't want this, not here and not now. I didn't want to lose my virginity on a desk. He grabbed my legs and pulled them apart and my heart pounded in my chest. Would he really penetrate me when I told him no?

"Vain I said no," I struggled against him.

"I just want to feel you, just for a minute. Let me put it in at least once. I promise I won't hurt you." I could hear the desperation in his voice as he pressed his lips against mine again.

He gripped my thigh tightly trying to keep my legs open. I placed my hands on his hips and tried to push him away from me. I didn't want this, and he knew that.

"STOP IT, STOP IT. I'M TELLING YOU NO!" I screamed shoving him away from me.

He shook his head and grabbed me slamming me down on the desk. I screamed when I heard

my shirt rip. He was really going to rape me.
This was really happening. He grabbed my legs
and ripped them open again. I wanted to give
up and just give in so that he would leave but I
didn't want to lose my virginity this way. I
looked at him and all I could see was lust and
anger. He looked like a monster, and it scared
me. When I felt him rub himself against my
entrance, I started to fight him again.

"VAIN PLEASE, PLEASE I JUST WANT TO
GO HOME. PLEASE STOP I DON'T WANT
THIS! YOU'RE HURTING ME!" I couldn't
stop the tears that escaped.

I hadn't even noticed that I was crying. My
body was shaking uncontrollably and all I could
do was beg him to stop. His eyes met mine and
he frowned taking a step back. I sat up and
instantly covered myself. I felt disgusted and I
blamed myself because I knew it was my fault.
I should have never allowed him to pleasure me
in the beginning. It was my fault, and I was so
stupid to give in to him.

"Shit," he mumbled. "I'm sorry Athena. I should have never…I don't know what happened." He reached for me, and I moved away from him quickly.

"Just get out," I sobbed softly. "I want you to leave…please."

He cursed under his breath and fixed his clothes quickly before leaving the room. After a few seconds, I heard the front door open and close. I jumped down from my desk and ran to lock the door. My body was still shaking, and I knew that I was still in shock. Once the door was locked, I sank down to the floor and hugged my knees to my chest. I could see my reflection in the mirror nearby and that made me cry harder. There was a bruise on my thigh from when he gripped me too hard. Hickey's that looked like bruises covered the left side of my neck. Scratches covered my skin from his nails. I looked a mess and the only thing I could do was sit there and cry.

Trust Lost

It had been a few days since I last saw Vain. I couldn't shake the fear that I still had. I was scared that night and he didn't even care. I left my dance studio around eleven and crept into the house. Roman wasn't home yet so I was able to shower and climb into bed without him seeing me. I knew that I had to cover up the hickeys. If he saw them, he would freak out and I didn't feel like reliving how I got them. I used makeup to cover up most of the damage, but there was so much that it was hard. I tapped my pencil on my notepad and stared at the chalkboard. The teacher was talking but I couldn't hear a word she was saying. The only thing that I could focus on was that night. I closed my eyes and put my head down on my desk. I couldn't even sleep these past few nights because I was having nightmares. It was so hard to shake my screams. I could still feel his hands gripping my thighs and his lips against my skin. I hated it more than anything. A part of me wanted to beg Roman for the money so that I wouldn't have to see Vain tomorrow. I took a deep breath and sat up slowly. Maybe I wouldn't go in on Saturday. I couldn't face him; I didn't want to. It was going to be hard to look him in the face after what he did to me. Even being in my dance studio didn't feel the same anymore. I stared out the window, what was I going to do?

The bell rang and I stood up quickly. I gathered my books and my bag and made my way to the door. The day was finally over, and I was grateful. The only thing that I wanted to do was go home and get in bed. I was supposed to have dance practice today, but I canceled. Everyone was happy about it because they don't like dancing on Fridays anyway. I walked out of the front door of the school and sighed. I was really starting to slack a lot and I hated it. I needed to get back to how I was before I met Vain. I couldn't let him take over my life and the things that I had going on.

"ATHENA, WAIT UP!"

I turned around and smiled when I saw Tarma running towards me. I loved my best friend but as of lately I have been dodging her too. I just needed to be alone so that I could heal properly. I wanted to talk to someone about it, but I knew that it wasn't a good idea.

"Hey, how are you?" I asked adjusting my bookbag.

She frowned, "what the hell is going on with you? You are so distant, and you never cancel dance practice. What is bothering you and don't try to lie to me." She folded her arms across her chest and stopped walking.

"I just haven't been sleeping well. I'm going to

go home and get some rest. I think that it's starting to mess me up but other than that I'm okay." I shrugged leaning against a light pole.

She cocked her head to the side, "who are you fooling? What is really going on?"

I shook my head, "I just told you. I'm not getting enough sleep. You can believe what you want but that's the truth."

"Okay, I'll step back. It's just you know I worry about you."

I grabbed her hand and squeezed it, "and I appreciate that. Trust me, if something was wrong, I would tell you. You don't have to worry about me. But besides me what have you been up to?"

She smiled, "just hanging with Ace. I think he and I need to make it official."

I looked over at her and raised an eyebrow, "are you sure about that?"

She stopped walking and sighed, "you're my

best friend and I can trust you, right?"

When did she start asking me dumb questions?
She had to know that any secret that she had
was safe with me. "Your secret is safe with me.
Whatever it is you know you can tell me."

She looked both ways and pulled me closer to
her, "I think that um…I think that I'm
pregnant."

I stared at her in complete shock. Did she say
what the hell I thought she said? Pregnant?
What the hell? I opened my mouth to speak but
no words came out. She shook her head and
sighed walking over to a nearby bench. I
wanted to comfort her, but I didn't know what
to say.

"How did…I mean what happened?"

She wiped away a few tears and shook her
head. "I don't know. I shouldn't have been so
stupid! I was so dumb to be reckless with him.
We started off using condoms and then he said
that he didn't want to. I told him that I wasn't

on the pill, and he promised me that he wouldn't cum in me. I'm three days late Athena and I'm freaking out."

I sighed, "it's okay I mean we all make mistakes. Does he want to be with you?" I grabbed her hand trying to comfort her the best way that I could.

She shook her head, "no. I saw him with another girl five days ago and we haven't spoken to each other."

"Men are such assholes," I mumbled. She sobbed softly and I rubbed her back trying to soother her. I knew that she was scared, and it made me feel bad that I haven't been here for her. "Have you taken a test?"

"No, I have been too afraid. What if it says that I'm pregnant, what will I do? I love dancing and I'm not ready to give that up. I can't take care of a baby by myself."

I kneeled down in front of her and made her look at me. "Listen, you will never be alone. No matter what, I'll always be here for you. I know that you're scared but we have to get a test. You have to take it because we have to know what our next step is going to be. If you want me to, I'll take it with you. I won't leave your side and you can come to my house."

She pulled me into a hug, "thank you."

"Anything for you," I smiled.

She walked out of the bathroom and sighed sitting down on my bed. I smiled at her and grabbed her hand. I wanted her to know that whatever the test said it didn't matter. She was not going to be alone. I was going to help her as much as I could, but I knew that she was worried about what she would have to give up. Being a mother was no joke and I didn't think that she was ready for that. I cleared my throat and grabbed my phone. The test said to wait about five minutes so now we were playing the waiting game.

"Are you sure you're okay? You know if you are having problems, you can tell me."

I looked up at her and smiled, "I'm fine. I'm just a little tired but I'll be fine."

"Will you go get the test and read the results. I don't think I can do it."

I nodded my head and climbed off the bed walking into the bathroom. I grabbed the pregnancy test off the sink and stared down at it. I smiled when I noticed that there was only one line on it. One line means that she wasn't pregnant. I walked into the room, and she looked up at me. I could see the fear in her eyes, but I knew that she would feel better once I told her the news.

"You're not pregnant," I smiled handing her the test.

"WHAT? REALLY OH MY GOD!" She screamed jumping up and grabbing the test from me. I shook my head and laughed at her. She was like a big baby when she wanted to be.

"Please be careful and always use a condom. Or don't have sex at all."

She placed a kiss on my cheek, "this makes me want to be like you. I can't afford a baby and I definitely learned my lesson. Thank goodness that I'm not stuck with him."

I laughed and watched her jump up and down. I was happy that she wasn't pregnant. I also realized that that's why I didn't want to have sex. Sex leads to babies and I didn't want any babies right now. Tarma grabbed her book bag and ran towards the door.

"I'll see you later, I'm supposed to be helping my dad today."

"Okay, I'll see you later. I'm going to take a nap so just lock the door behind you." She smiled and walked out of my room closing the door behind her. I didn't waste any time climbing into my bed and snuggling under the covers. I was exhausted and I could barely keep my eyes open any longer. I smiled and allowed my heavy eyelids to fall closed. Hopefully, I wouldn't have a nightmare this time.

"WHAT THE HELL IS THIS? ATHENA WAKE THE FUCK UP NOW!"

I groaned and rolled over when I heard Roman yelling. Why was he yelling? What was his problem now?

"I didn't leave my bookbag on the floor," I mumbled half asleep.

"I'M NOT TALKING ABOUT YOUR DAMN BOOKBAG. WHAT THE HELL IS A

PREGNANCY TEST DOING IN THE HOUSE?"

I sat up quickly when he said something about a pregnancy test. Tarma was supposed to take that with her, but she didn't. Now Roman was in here yelling at me because he thought that it was mine.

"That's not mine."

He rolled his eyes, "do you think I'm stupid? Who the hell lives here besides you and me? I don't take pregnancy tests, Athena. Stop fucking lying to me or I swear to god."

"ROMAN IT'S NOT MINE!"

"THEN WHO DOES IT BELONG TO?" he screamed back at me.

"It's Tarma's." I didn't want to put her business on blast because I promised to keep it a secret. But I wasn't about to allow Roman to think that it was me. He wouldn't trust me ever again.

He looked at me and frowned, "what the hell do

you mean? Are you saying that she took a test at our house?"

"Yes, look I'm not supposed to be telling anyone. Please just keep this to yourself. She thought that she was pregnant but she's not."

He shook his head, "this is why I don't want you hanging out with her. She is a bad influence, and this is proof. She has been having sex since she was fourteen years old. Athena, I don't want you around her anymore. She is no longer a part of your dance crew, and her parents will know about this."

I shook my head, "you can't do that!"

"I can and I will. I refuse to allow you to turn out like her. Most of all I'm not about to have her problems fall back on me. If her parents catch wind of this, they will come after me. I'm going to tell them and I'm sorry, but you can't be her friend. If you disobey me, I will take away dancing for you completely."

My heart was shattering with every word he

was saying. Was he really going to take away the only friend that I truly had? "Roman, you can't do this! She is the only true friend that I have! The dance tournament is coming up and we have been practicing for weeks. You can't mess this up now!"

He sighed, "I'm sorry Athena. I stand by what I said. I don't want you around her anymore. I know that she is fucking Ace. He is Vain's, right-hand man. Anything can happen to you because she is dealing with the enemy. I'm not risking your safety. You can hate me, I don't care. But this can't go on. All these late nights that you're having these days. I don't know what you're doing. From now on, I want you in the house by nine o clock. I will hire security and make them drag you in the house if I have to."

"You're being too overprotective Roman. You can't just shelter me like this."

"I lost mom and dad. I won't lose you too," he walked out of my room and closed the door.

I sat there and tried to breathe even though I couldn't. I was losing my one and only friend. Not only that but I was now on a curfew. What the hell was I going to do?

I'm Sorry

I was nervous to see Vain today. I didn't want
to see his face, but I knew I had to face him. I
had to tell him about the curfew that my brother
put me on. Roman was pissed off last night but
I was able to talk to him today. I told him that
on Saturday's I practiced late, and I got him to
agree to eleven o clock. I knew that Vain would
be upset but I didn't care. I couldn't disobey my
brother. I looked up at the sky and I adjusted
my bag on my shoulder. I was headed to the
club to start my shift. I wouldn't be able to stick
around tonight but they would be fine. I had a

lot of other things on my mind apart from Vain.
Roman called Tarma's parents and told them
about what happened. He also told them that he
didn't want her in my dance crew anymore. I
was heartbroken but most of all I felt like I
betrayed her. I knew that I would have to face
her at school, and I didn't want to. What was I
going to say to her? She loved dancing just as
much as I did and now, she couldn't even dance
with me anymore. Not only that but I would
have to redo the whole dance because we no
longer had her. There was so much stuff on my
mind, and I still had to show my face tonight. I
rounded the corner and rolled my eyes when I
saw the club come into view. I would be lying
if I said that my heart started beating a little
faster.

"ATHENA!"

I turned around and smiled when I saw Tarma
running towards me. It was nice to see her face.
I wanted to make things right with her and tell
her what happened. She stopped in front of me

and placed her hand on her hip.

"Why the hell did you tell your brother about me? Because of you, my parents are making me move to California."

I stared at her in shock. What the hell was her problem? I mean I knew that she was upset but I didn't think she would talk to me crazy. I thought that she would understand why I told him.

"You act like I told him willingly. He came at me yelling at me because you left your test in the house. He thought it was mine, what was I supposed to do?"

She rolled her eyes, "be a good fucking friend. Take up for me and say it was yours. What do you mean, I would have done it for you?"

I looked at her and laughed. She had to be joking, "you're joking, right? You want me to say that a pregnancy test is mine? Listen to yourself, okay. You know Roman better than anyone. If I would have told him that it belonged to me then I wouldn't even be able to leave the house."

"Boo freaking who Athena. You are pitiful."

I frowned and crossed my arms over my chest. "I'm pitiful because I didn't lie about having sex and thinking I was pregnant. Dude, you're insane. I don't want to argue with you about this. I know what I did was right and it's not my fault that you were being reckless."

She laughed, "at least I know how to live. You are a boring human being Athena. You act like you're such an innocent little virgin, but we all know the truth. You are a total slut, and it shows. Everyone at school talks about you and even the people in our crew. That night at the club you let Vain fuck you and instead of being honest about it, you lied."

What the hell was she talking about? I had never had sex with Vain, where was she getting this from? "You are crazy," I mumbled turning my back to her.

"Yea, run away like you always do."

I shook my head and turned to face her. "I'm not running away. I just refuse to stand here and be lied on. I never touched Vain and the fact that you accuse me of that is disgusting. You always try to put your insecurities off on me Tarma and it isn't fair."

"I'm far from insecure, Athena."

I rolled my eyes, "Sure you are. If that was the case me being a virgin wouldn't bother you. You wouldn't keep throwing it in my face or trying to make me lose it. You literally throw men at me that I don't want. You tell them to try to sleep with me and I have let it go on for too long. I was just trying to be an understanding friend, but I don't understand you."

She walked towards me and pushed me. "The only reason that I befriended you was because no one wanted to be your friend. You are weak and afraid of everything Roman says. You can't

even live without going to him and bowing
down to him. Your dancing sucks and that's
why we haven't won a tournament yet. But do I
say all this stuff to you? No, I don't because
I'm a good friend. I spare your feelings and I
try to be by your side. I have your back when
no one does, even our dance crew. Even your
own brother. Your brother had sex with me, and
I hid it to protect you. Remember the nights I
would stay over because I wanted girl time with
you? I was only doing that so that I could have
sex with Roman. He got me pregnant, and I lost
the baby. That's the only reason that he wants
to get rid of me."

Was I hearing her right? She had sex with my
brother, and they just kept this from me? She
was only around because of him. She never
gave a damn about me. I balled my hands into
fists and pushed her back. "It's not my fault that
you're a slut Tarma. You fuck anything that
walks just for his attention. And you wonder
why Ace grew bored with you. Yea I might not
live a lot but at least I'm not a whore. Half of

the city has been with you. You try to make all your problems mine and they are not! I'm sorry that your stepbrother raped you when you were twelve. I'm sorry that you crave attention from men just to feel the void inside you. You need therapy because letting men screw you isn't enough. And it's not our crew, it's my crew."

Tears came to her eyes and she balled up her fists. "I don't ever want you to talk to me again."

She turned around and ran away from me. I stood there and I couldn't help but instantly regret what I said. I knew that she was trying to hurt my feelings because of what Roman did. But I wasn't about to take her abuse. I knew that I did nothing wrong by covering my ass and telling my brother the truth, I didn't deserve to be treated like this. I looked down at my phone and cursed under my breath. It was seven o clock, I had to go get ready for tonight. I walked towards the club quickly because I didn't want to be seen. When I reached the door, I stepped in and sighed. I couldn't even think straight right now but I had to put it behind me. I bit my lip and walked towards the stairs quickly. I needed to talk to Vain, the sooner the better. I knew that I had to face him, there was no way around that. I jogged up the stairs towards his office. When I reached the top, I took a deep breath and knocked on his office door. The door was closed so I didn't want to just walk in. I heard him say come in and I pushed the door open. Roxy was sitting on the edge of his desk, and he was staring down at his phone. When he looked up and saw me, he sat up quickly.

"What can I help you with?"

"I wanted to talk to you about something." I looked at Roxy and she smirked placing her hand on Vain's shoulder. I guess she was thinking that I was going to talk with her in the room.

He cleared his throat, "Roxy give me and baby doll a minute."

She stared at him in disbelief, but she didn't fight with him. She stood up and walked out of his office quickly. When the door slammed behind her, I turned my attention back to Vain. I was nervous once again, but I knew that I couldn't be. I had to show him that I wasn't afraid of him, and he couldn't scare me.

"So, what is it?" He mumbled looking back down at his phone.

"My brother put me on a curfew. So, I have to be in the house by eleven on Saturdays."

He looked up at me, "I know what happened. Your little friend had a pregnancy scare with Ace."

I stared at him confused, "wait how did you know that?"

"Ace is my best friend, he told me. He said that her dad confronted him, and her dad said that he got a call from Roman Vintalli about a pregnancy test being found in his house."

I nodded my head slowly, "yea. That pretty much sums it up. Roman is angry right now and I just want to give him what he's asking for. I know it won't last long but he's upset."

He took a deep breath, "I won't be paying you the full amount. I'll only be paying you a thousand dollars. I will take my portion out of that."

"That's fine," I turned to leave but I heard him stand up.

"Athena, I wanted to tell you that I'm sorry. I never meant to hurt you," he walked towards me, and I stepped back.

"Vain."

I tried to avoid him, but he grabbed my hand and pulled me to him. "I know that you don't believe me, and I know that you're scared of me. But I want you to know that I would never rape a woman. I may be a lot of things, but I would never do that. I was drinking that night and so things got a little out of hand. If I hurt you in any way, I'm truly sorry and I want to make it up to you."

I looked into his eyes and all I could see was regret. He shocked me that night because he had never done that before. The night that we met in the club he didn't force himself on me. When I told him to stop, he did. I knew that he had to be telling the truth about drinking because he had never acted like that before.

I licked my lips, "I'll think about it."

He smiled but that smile quickly faded. He reached for my hair and moved it away from my neck. "Did I do this?" He whispered brushing his fingers along the hickeys he left on my skin.

"Yeah," I looked down at my feet.

He cursed under his breath and shook his head. "You don't have to work tonight. I'll give you your full pay. I'll take you home so that you can rest."

I didn't want any special treatment. The last thing I wanted was the other girls to think that I was getting special treatment. "No, I can stay and work. I'm not in any pain or anything."

He shook his head, "not tonight. I want you to rest."

I sighed and nodded my head. If that's what he wanted, then I was willing to give him that. The last thing I wanted to do was argue with him. He grabbed his keys and smirked.

"You said that your curfew was eleven tonight, right?"

"Yeah."

He smiled, "how about we take a detour. We have plenty of time."

I frowned, "what kind of detour?"

He laughed and grabbed my hand, "you'll see. I get to show you how sorry I am, and I get to show you a good time. I think tonight is going to be fun."

"What about the club? Don't you have to stay here and keep things running?" I didn't know if he could just leave. What if something went wrong?

He shrugged, "I'll have Ace watch over things. I want to spend tonight with you." He wrapped his arm around my shoulder, and we walked towards the door. What did he have planned for tonight?

Sii Mio

I stared out the car window and sighed. Vain
didn't tell me where we were going and so it
was nerve-racking. He said that I would have
fun but how could I trust that? He turned the
radio down, but I didn't pay him any attention.
My mind was still on Tarma. I hated that she
was moving to California. It sucked that we
were going to end things on bad terms. That's
the last thing that I wanted to do with her. I
never meant to hurt her feelings or make her
cry, but I couldn't forget the things she said to
me. She said that everyone knew that I had
slept with Vain. But who? She said the dance
crew, but they never mentioned it to me. Were
they talking about me behind my back? Was

that really a rumor that was going around or did she just say that to upset me? My brother was a filthy liar, and I didn't want to talk to him at the moment. I rolled my eyes; I was pissed off. It was hard to try to enjoy myself when they upset me so bad.

"What's wrong?"

I turned my attention to Vain, "what do you mean?"

He smiled, "something seems to be bothering you. Do you want to talk about it?"

I shook my head and turned my attention back towards the window. "Not really. I don't think that it will help anyway."

"You don't know if you don't try. I would rather you talk about it and get it off your chest. I would hate to see you in a bad mood the whole night."

I didn't want to talk about it but maybe he was right. I needed another person's point of view on the situation. I needed to know if I was wrong for telling Roman the truth. "Earlier today Tarma came up to me and she was upset. She was upset because her parents are making her move to California and she thinks it's my fault."

He frowned, "why would that be your fault?"

"Well, you know she left her pregnancy test in my house, right? My brother found it and he instantly thought it was mine. I tried to reason with him and tell him that it wasn't, but he didn't believe me. He wanted to know who it belonged to and so I told him. He got upset and told me that he didn't want me to be around her, and he didn't want her dancing with me anymore. When she confronted me today, she said some pretty horrible things to me."

"Like what?" He asked interrupting me.

"She said that everyone knew that I was a slut. Everyone knows that I had sex with you. Which is not true at all. She talked about my dancing and so I fired back. I said some hurtful stuff to her, but I was just upset. I know that I shouldn't have let her get to me, but she was acting as if it was my fault. I just feel confused, and I beat myself up for it." I left out my brother having sex with her for now. That was a topic that I knew would make me cry and I didn't want to cry.

He shook his head, "you did the right thing. You didn't want to take the bullet for something you didn't do. A real friend wouldn't ask you to do that, Athena. A real friend would take ownership of their actions. They can't hide behind the backs of other people and that is what she was trying to do. If she can't understand that then she isn't a real friend."

I smiled at him, and he smiled back. He was right, she wasn't a real friend. Regardless of what happened, she should have never talked about me like that. She should have never gotten angry with me because I didn't take the bullet for her. Vain was pretty sweet once you got to know him. Well, he had his good days. It seemed like tonight would probably be a good day with him. He turned his attention back to the road and I smiled staring straight ahead.

"I hope I can get your mind off your friend tonight."

I laughed, "where are we going?"

"It's a surprise and we are almost there anyway. So, sit back and enjoy the ride."

I looked at him and shook my head. What did this man have planned?

We pulled up to a huge lake and I smiled. There in front of the lake was a helicopter. I had never seen one this close up before, so it amazed me. Vain climbed out of the car and walked around the car to open my door. I thanked him and climbed out of the car slowly. What the hell were we doing here? He walked towards the helicopter, and I followed him quickly. It was dark outside, and I didn't want to get lost. He turned around and laughed when he saw me struggling to catch up to him. I was about to ask him what he was laughing at, but he silenced me by lifting me into his arms. He carried me bridal style towards the helicopter, and I stared at it in amazement. What on earth did this man have planned?

"Tonight, I am going to take you on your first helicopter ride."

I stared at him in shock, "you're going to fly this?"

"Yeah, I've been flying for seven years. You don't have to worry; I'll have you back home safe and sound." He set me down on my feet and I took a deep breath watching him open the door for me.

I hesitated but climbed in quickly admiring the inside of it. He walked around to his side and climbed in smiling at me. I shook my head and placed my trembling hands in my lap. I was terrified, not of heights but of him driving this thing. We were going to be thousands of feet up in the air and he was going to be in control of my life.

"Trust me, I'll keep you safe." He grabbed my seat belt and pulled it across my lap. I looked down at his hands that happened to be too close to my vagina. He didn't pay much attention because he grabbed the seat belt that went across my chest and strapped it into the middle section. He made sure that I was in tight and then he strapped himself in. I stared out the window admiring the scenery. It was beautiful here; I could only imagine what it looked like during the day. I turned towards Vain, and he handed me a headset that I quickly put on. He did the same and then started clicking on buttons. The helicopter slowly started to come to life and so did my heartbeat. He spoke into the microphone that he was ready to depart, and a voice came back and said copy that. I bit my lip and closed my eyes as I felt the helicopter slowly start to move.

"Don't close your eyes. You'll miss a lot if you do."

I opened my eyes, and I could feel the butterflies flying around in my stomach. We were getting higher and higher. I was scared because his car kept getting smaller and smaller until I couldn't see it anymore. I gulped and turned to look at him, but he wasn't paying attention to me. His eyes were straight ahead, and I guess that was a good thing. I giggled and stared out the window as we hovered over the lake.

"Are you ready to see the city from up in the sky."

My eyes widened, "yes. I would love to."

"Good," he chuckled.

We started to fly away from the lake, and I could only look out the window in amazement. I never thought that I would get in a helicopter. I was afraid of flying because of all the plane crashes that I heard about. I knew that I would always wish to do it but never have the guts to do it. I looked over at Vain again, I was doing this with him. It felt kind of nice to feel safe and be having fun at the same time.

"The city is coming up."

I looked in front of me and my eyes lit up when I saw the city from where we were. It was beautiful from up here. The tall buildings were lit up and the streets were crowded with cars. Even though the cars looked like ants from up here it was still beautiful. I would never look at the city the same now that I got to see it like this. It was an amazing feeling and most of all it sparked something in me. Vain kept driving and all I could do was look out and go crazy about every little thing I saw.

"Do you want to go higher?"

I nodded my head quickly and he chuckled. I screamed and laughed as the butterflies in my stomach flew around in a frenzy. My heart was pounding but I loved it. I loved looking down at the city as it got smaller and smaller the higher, we got. This night was magical, and it was one I would remember forever.

Vain pulled into my driveway and I smiled at him. Roman sent me a text message at ten-thirty and asked if I was on my way home. I knew that he wasn't playing about this curfew thing. I pulled out my phone and sent Roman a quick text saying that I was home. Vain smiled at me and I returned the smile. Tonight, wasn't so bad even though I spent it with him.

"You have ten more minutes before you have to go inside."

I laughed and shook my head, "that's not funny. I feel like a child sometimes."

He shrugged, "He has his reasons trust me. If I had a little sister as beautiful as you, I would be overprotective too."

"Why are you an only child?" I was curious to know why his parents didn't have any more kids. They were probably young when they had Vain, so why did they stop?

"My father didn't want any children. The lifestyle he lived in was not one that you would bring a child into. When I was born, he wasn't around a lot. He made my mother and I live in Spain by ourselves. Then when I was six, he brought us here and started to teach me about the mafia. When we came here my parents fought all the time, so they didn't do a lot of lovemaking. My father was a cheater, and he didn't love my mother. He didn't know how to love her. He only cheated on her and she eventually left him and went back to Spain

when I was fourteen. So, that left me
motherless for four years. When I turned
eighteen my father handed his job over to me
and left to get her back."

I looked down at my hands, "I see." It was sad
to hear that his parents fought a lot. He was
without his mom for four years and had to go
through being split up again. I couldn't imagine
that happening to me if my parents were still
alive.

"What about you?"

I sighed, "my parents loved each other. My
father never cheated on my mother. They had
renewed their wedding vows and were going
out to celebrate. But they died that night."

He placed his hand on my shoulder, "I hate that
you lost them."

"Thank you," I whispered tucking a strand of
hair behind my ear. Silence surrounded us once
again and I bit my lip nervously. "Do you want
children?" I wanted to know if he felt the same
way that his father did. I know that it was
random, but I was curious.

He chuckled, "no. I don't want any children. They are a handful and I know that I don't have the time for a child."

"Everyone has their reasons," I smiled reaching for the doorknob.

He grabbed my hand and placed a kiss on it, "Sii Mio."

I shook my head and laughed. I didn't know what that meant, and I hated when he spoke another language. "Well, I have to go but I enjoyed tonight. Thank you," I leaned over and placed a kiss on his cheek before climbing out the car. I walked towards my front door and pulled my key out. I made it home before my brother which was a good thing. I pushed the key in the lock and turned it. I heard Vain's car pulling away as I pushed my front door open.

Lunch Date

I rounded the corner and smiled when I saw
Vain standing there holding flowers. I laughed
tucking a strand of hair behind my ear. What
was he doing? We were only supposed to be
going to get lunch. I didn't know that this was
supposed to be a date. He smiled at me, and I
couldn't help but check him out. He was
leaning against the building. He had on a black
suit with a black undershirt. His hair never
failed to be anything but neat. Strangely, he was
always in business attire, but it made sense. He
was a mafia leader, and he was running a

business. I looked down at my attire and frowned. I wore a yellow sundress that was decorated with mini black hearts. I decided to wear my all-white vans to match with it. I mentally slapped myself, why didn't I dress nicer? I took a deep breath and forced a smile as I neared Vain. When we were standing face to face, he handed me the flowers. I cleared my throat and thanked him softly. I loved flowers and I had never gotten flowers from a guy before. So, this was the first...he was the first. He said that he wanted to take me out to lunch but he didn't say where. I was hoping that it wouldn't be crowded wherever he decided to take me.

"You look lovely?"

I stared up at him in shock, "oh...um thank you. You look nice as well. I didn't know where we were going so, I wore something simple."

He laughed, "I wouldn't call that simple." He offered me his arm and I took it.

I had dance practice later so I couldn't stay with him long. I think that he had something to do today as well. We walked in silence, and I didn't mind. I needed time to think about what was going on. I kept telling myself that I should stay away from him, but I kept finding my way back. I agreed to go to lunch with him and I instantly regretted it. I guess it was something about him that I liked. Maybe it had nothing to do with me. He was good at drawing women in and maybe that is what he was doing to me. After this, I had to try to put some distance between us. If I only saw him on Saturdays, then it wouldn't be so bad.

"I can only spend an hour with you today. I'm sorry, I have a very important meeting to go to."

I nodded my head quickly, "it's fine. I have dance practice at two o clock."

We walked towards a restaurant called Greek Valley. It was a restaurant that had statues of the Greek gods surrounding the building. The path to the front door was decorated as if it was a valley. I heard of the restaurant, but I had never been. Vain pointed towards an eating area outside and I smiled. It was such a nice day, and I was happy that we would be able to enjoy the sun. He pulled my chair out for me and I thanked him. He nodded his head and took his seat across from me. I grabbed the menu that was sitting in front of me and started to flip through it. I was starving, I skipped breakfast to have an appetite when I came with him. I could feel Vain staring at me, and it was bugging me. I looked up and frowned and he laughed at my response.

"What's so funny?"

He smiled, "you don't like being stared at?"

"I don't think anyone would," I laughed rolling my eyes.

A waitress came up to us and she smiled. "Mr. Grey, I see you're back again."

I could tell that she was flirting with him, and

it irritated me. Women were always throwing themselves at him. Did they have no self-respect at all? I mean it was pathetic that women made it so easy for him to have sex with them. Well in my words, use them. That's all he was doing was using them for sex. He didn't love them, and he never would.

He chuckled, "dammi il solito. What will you be having?"

The waitress stared at me and frowned. It was as if she was just noticing that I was here. "I'll have the Goddess of love Lemonade with the loaded greek fries"

I handed her my menu and she smirked snatching it from me. She turned back to Vain and leaned over him to take his menu. Vain cleared his throat and stared at me to avoid staring at her chest, which was too close to his face. When she walked away I shook my head. She was so pathetic and it showed.

I frowned, "when did you learn to speak another language?"

"It's Italian. My mother doesn't speak English so Italian is the first language that I learned. When I came to America, I had to learn English of course."

"I see." I smiled at our waitress when she placed our drinks on the table. She said that our food would be ready in ten minutes before walking away. I took a sip of my drink and smiled looking around.

"Do you know any language besides English?"

I shook my head, "no. My mother was Korean and she was teaching me but I didn't learn fluently. I know the basics to have a conversation."

He laughed, "I gotcha. What got you into dance?"

I looked up shocked that he asked. No one had ever asked why I loved dancing. Not even Roman, he didn't show any interest when it came to my dancing. "Well, my mom said that I was always dancing. Even as a child, I would dance around the house. I guess it's just something that I grew up doing. It's a part of who I am and I feel complete when I'm dancing. It seems like since my parents died I've been dancing a lot more. My mom used to tell me all the time to chase my dreams."

"I'm shocked that your brother doesn't support you. I mean you're not like all these other girls out here. He should at least be happy about that."

I shook my head, "what do you mean by other girls?"

He shrugged, "you're not having sex. You're not clubbing and getting drunk or doing drugs. You're a good girl, Athena. He should be proud of that and he shouldn't try to take away your dreams."

I smiled, "I think he is coming around. I know he just wants the best for me." Although I was still upset with Roman I knew that he was accepting me dancing.

The waitress came back carrying our food and my face lit up. I was so hungry and the food smelled amazing. She asked us if there was anything else we needed and Vain said no. She took one last look at me before walking away and leaving us alone. I grabbed my fork and started to eat my food quickly. Loaded fries were always my favorite and these were amazing.

"I want to take you to an island for two days. It's located in Spain and I have a condo there that I own. "

I looked up at Vain and frowned, "I can't. There's no way that I can get away from my brother for two days. Besides, I have dance practice. I can't just leave my crew hanging."

"Come on, it'll be fun. We can leave on Saturday and come back Monday."

I took a deep breath, "I'll think about it. Can I text you tonight with my answer."

He smirked, "yes."

I bit my lip and smiled, "good."

I walked into my house quickly. I had to get changed so that I could meet my crew at the studio. I had a good time with Vain and the food was amazing. He told me a few stories about his life and what Spain was like. It was nice to see this different side of him. Even though he was still the same old Vain at times. I ran towards the stairs but Roman called my name. I stopped and turned around quickly to see him walking towards me. What did he want? I didn't get to talk to him about what Tarma said to me. I was upset but most of all I was hurt. I never thought that he would do that to me. I never thought that he would lie to me.

"Can we talk?"

I nodded my head, "yea. Why don't you tell me why you were having sex with Tarma? Did you really get her pregnant? Were you doing that behind my back?"

He stared at me in shock, "Athena let me explain."

I crossed my arms over my chest waiting for
him to speak. I wanted to know why he
betrayed me like that.

"I never meant for it to go that far."

Tears came to my eyes, "were you jealous that
she was with Ace? Is that why you told her
parents? Did it hurt you that maybe she could
be pregnant by another man after she lost your
child?"

He frowned walking towards me, "I don't give
a damn about her. The only person that I care
about is you. Listen to me, I fucked up Athena.
I came home drunk and she was in the kitchen.
I tried to go to my room but she stopped me and
pulled her nightgown off. One thing led to
another and I woke up next to her. She got
pregnant from that one night but I never fucked
her again. I paid the little slut off so that she
could keep her mouth closed. The money
wasn't enough and I should have known that.
She became infatuated with me and I didn't
want her and because of that she said that she
would tell you."

I closed my eyes and sobbed softly. I couldn't
process all this information. Most of all I
couldn't help but feel heartbroken. I knew that
Roman would never hurt me on purpose but I
was upset that he never told me what was going
on. Why did he keep it from me if she was
blackmailing him?

"Why didnt you just tell me what was going
on?"

He closed his eyes and ran his fingers through
his hair. "Because she was your friend. You
were finally close to someone and I didn't want
to take that away from you. You didn't talk to
me for months after mom and dad died. You
talked to her though and she was able to make
you laugh. How could I take that away from
you? Besides, this happened last year. I thought
it would just go away."

I wiped away my tears, "how much did you pay
her?"

"Athena."

"HOW MUCH DID YOU PAY HER?" I wanted to know how much money he gave her to stay silent.

He cursed under his breath, "I paid her twenty-five thousand dollars."

I stared at him and shook my head in disbelief. "It hurts me that you paid her money that I had been asking for. I asked you to help me buy a dance studio and I didn't get a dime. You would rather invest your money into your mistakes than in my dreams. I hate you...I never thought that I would say that. I wish mom and dad were still here," I whispered before running up the stairs.

Humiliating me like that and making me look like a fool was hurtful. She was walking around with money for the dance studio that I was looking at every day. She was no friend, she was a whore. She did anything she could to get money from men and I was glad that she was gone. I couldn't sit in this house like this. I didn't want to be around Roman right now. I needed some time to think and now going to Spain sounded like a good idea. I pulled my phone out of my pocket and pulled up Vain's number. I typed the text into the message field and debated with myself on sending it. I bit my lip and closed my eyes pressing the send button. I looked down when my phone buzzed. He had texted me back.

12:11

V

Vain >

Text Message
Today 12:05 PM

Spain sounds nice

Is that a yes, amore?

Yea...but can we leave tomorrow?

What's wrong !?

I just need to get away for a while that's all

We can leave tonight if that will make you happy.

🤍 yes please

Text Message

Innocence Tainted

We walked towards the front door of the condo. I stared at it in amazement because it was beautiful. The beach condo wasn't right on the beach, but it was pretty close to it. It was a two-story condo that looked like a house. Vain took my bags and I smiled pushing open the front door after he unlocked it. The inside was just as beautiful as the outside. I climbed the steps quickly trying to get a better view of the upstairs. Vain yelled something but I couldn't hear him from where I was. I walked into the bedroom and my jaw dropped. There was a huge bed in the middle of the room. There was no mistaking it's size, it was a California king bed. I laughed and dived stomach first on to the bed. This place was amazing, I was glad that I came. I never got to go anywhere and Roman never took me anywhere nice. I was always either at home or at school and that was getting bored. Vain walked into the room and I smiled at him. I was eager to see what Spain had to offer.

"Do you like it?"

I stared at him confused, "are you kidding. I freaking love it. This place is amazing."

He laughed, "it better be. This place cost me sixty thousand dollars."

My mouth flew open, "that's crazy. I would never pay that much for anything."

He laughed, "money is nothing. I make about sixty thousand dollars every hour. I just need someone to share it with."

I shook my head, "you have a lot of people to share it with. What are we going to do today? I want to get out and see what all this place has to offer."

He chuckled, "it's one in the morning. We need to get some rest and then we can explore tomorrow."

I rolled my eyes, "I guess."

He shook his head, "I'm going to take a shower. So, you get comfortable, and I'll see you in a minute."

I nodded my head and grabbed the remote to the tv and climbed in the bed. I was wide awake and now I was stuck in here with him. I rolled my eyes and grabbed my phone. This was going to be a long night. I grabbed my headphones out of my bag and put them in my ear. I turned to my favorite song by BoA and started to sing along. I flipped through the movies on Netflix hoping that I would find something interesting to watch. There was this one movie that I had my eye on, but Tarma never wanted to watch it. I sighed and ran my fingers through my hair. Here I was thinking about her. I took a deep breath and placed the remote on the pillow beside me. I had to go use the bathroom, I had been holding it for a while. I yanked my headphones out and left my phone on the bed as I rushed to the bathroom. I pushed the door open, and I instantly regretted barging in because Vain was naked. He was in the shower, and I could see every inch of his body. I hid around the corner and closed my eyes. How in the hell did I forget he was in here? I hit myself on the head and rolled my eyes. I peeked around the corner and watched him. I knew that it was wrong, but he was so damn sexy. I watched him as he washed his chest and then his stomach. The lower his hands got the lower my eyes went. I bit my lip and squeezed my legs together watching him stroke himself. He opened his eyes quickly and my eyes widened as I ducked my head back around the corner. I head the water turn off and I cursed under my breath running back into the bedroom. I grabbed my headphones and placed them back in my ear pretending to look on my phone. He walked into the room with a towel around his waist.

"Athena."

I looked up at him and smiled pausing my song. "Hey, how was your shower."

He laughed looking me up and down, "it was fine. It would have been better if you were there."

I cocked my head to the side, "so I guess we will just sleep then?"

He sat down on the bed, "I want you to be honest with me about something. Why did you want to leave tonight? What had you so upset?"

I looked down at my hands and sighed, "it's my brother. I told him that I hated him because of something he did."

He frowned moving closer to me, "what did he do?"

"He had sex with Tarma. He got her pregnant, but she lost the baby. This whole time I thought that he was trying to protect me, but he was fooling me. I never thought that he would do that to me."

"Wait he fucked your best friend? How did you find out?"

I looked into his eyes, "the day that you to took

158

me for a helicopter ride. When she confronted me, she told me everything."

"Do you think that she might be saying that stuff to get you mad at your brother?" He shrugged.

I shook my head, "no. I asked my brother today and he didn't deny it." A tear slid down my cheek, "he said that it only happened one time and he was drunk. He said that he tried to walk away but she got naked, and one thing led to another. He paid her hush money to stay silent, but she grew obsessed with him. I don't know what to believe Vain, I just feel so confused. I left him a note and I didn't even tell him where I was going." I sobbed softly because I needed to get it out. This whole time I've been trying to pretend like I was okay, but I wasn't. I was hurting and I couldn't hide it anymore.

He pulled me into his arms and held me as I cried. I could hear him whispering that it was okay, but it wasn't. I told Roman that I hated him and that was eating me up. He pulled away and wiped away my tears forcing me to look at him.

"I know that it's hurting you and I don't want to see you sad. Just tell me how I can help."

I wrapped my arms around his neck pulling him into a hug. "Tell me what I should do."

He pulled me into his lap, "I think that you should give him a chance to explain himself. I'm not taking up for him, but I know what it's like to be drunk. Women take advantage of you and that is the only thing that I can vouch for him on. Tarma is pretty clingy, I heard that from Ace. Other than that, he should have been honest with you. Especially about him paying her off. If anything, he should have just bought the dance studio for you."

I took a deep breath and wiped away my tears, "I love him. I just don't know how to forgive him."

He cupped my chin forcing me to look at him, "you will. Just give it time and you will open your heart up to him. You're just upset right now and that is understandable." He leaned forward pressing his lips against mine. This kiss was not a kiss full of lust. It was a passionate kiss filled with need. He needed to feel the void in me, and I felt the same way. Our lips moved in sync with each other and that only made me want him more. He pulled my bottom lip between his teeth and groaned grinding himself into my core. I wanted him but I knew that I wasn't ready. I moaned when he attacked my neck with kisses. My mind was telling me no, but my body was begging him to continue. I closed my eyes and bit my lip placing my hand on his chest.

"Vain."

He looked into my eyes and shook his head. "Don't stop me now. I can't wait anymore, Athena. Just let me make you feel good. Let me take away all your pain. I won't hurt you... I promise." He laid me down on the bed and climbed on top of me. He parted my legs with his knee and all I could do was watch him.

A part of me wanted this and I was tired of fighting it. I was tired of being told what to do all the time. This was my decision to make and mine alone. I wanted Vain more than anything. I couldn't handle pushing him away anymore.

He grabbed my shirt and pulled it over my
head. I wanted to cover myself, but I closed my
eyes and forced myself not to. "You're so damn
beautiful," he whispered unhooking my bra. I
bit my lip and moaned loudly when his mouth
sucked at my flesh. He looked up at me and
smirked swirling his tongue around my right
nipple. He was taking his time with me, and I
was glad for that.

He kissed down my stomach slowly and I
watched him in amazement. He looked into my
eyes and slid my shorts and panties down at the
same time. His eyes never left mine as he
spread my legs. I knew what he was about to
do, and I was ready for it. When his mouth
connected with my core, I arched my back and
moaned loudly. I gripped the pillow for support
as his licks became relentless. His tongue
thrashed and stroked my sensitive bud. All I
could do was grip the blanket on the bed and
beg for more. The feeling in my stomach was
building up and I knew that I was close I
needed this release and I only hoped that he
wouldn't rob me of it. The sound of him
devouring me was driving me crazy. I begged
him not to stop as my stomach started to

constrict. My legs started to shake, and my moans grew louder as my orgasm neared its peak. I screamed his name and threw my head back as tiny sparks flew threw me.

"Vain, oh...please," I screamed as he held me down. He groaned and continued to slurp up the remnants of my juices.

He chuckled and pulled away his towel. My eyes trailed down to his erection and I bit my lip. I needed to let go just for tonight. I needed to live and be free instead of being boring. He climbed between my legs, and I closed my eyes and moaned when he rubbed himself against me.

"Tell me you want this," he groaned staring into my eyes.

"I want this," I whispered.

He cursed under his breath and brought his lips to my neck once again. I moaned softly and placed my hands on his chest. He was perfect in every way. He smiled and once again brought his lips down to meet mine. I opened my mouth, and he wasted no time sucking on my tongue. I could feel him rubbing himself against me and it was turning me on even more.

"You're so wet to be a virgin" he whispered breaking the kiss. "Are you ready?"

I nodded my head slowly. I was nervous but I didn't want to turn back. I wanted to know what sex felt like. I wanted to fit in with everyone else. I was going to prove to Tarma that I wasn't boring. I looked down and watched as he aligned himself with my entrance. My heart was pounding in my chest and my brain was screaming at me. I was nervous and scared. I was nervous about how I would feel after this, and I was scared because I knew it would be painful. He closed his eyes and prepared to enter me, but I put my hand on his chest to stop him.

"Wait...don't you need a condom?"

He looked into my eyes and sighed. "No, I want to feel you. It's your first time and I want us to enjoy it." Before I could protest, he kissed me roughly and I whimpered feeling him start to enter me. He broke the kiss and groaned burying his face in my neck.

"Vain…ouch," I closed my eyes tight.

"Relax," that's all he said before sucking my nipple into his mouth. I stared up at the ceiling and tried to relax but the pain was overwhelming. I put my hand on his chest again when I felt him push inside me. He didn't stop and so I pushed against his chest in an attempt to slow him down. He took a deep breath and pushed my legs open when I tried to close them. I stared into his eyes and all I could see was lust.

"Vain it hurts," I whispered with tears in my eyes.

He grabbed my hands and pinned them above my head. "I know, but it will feel better. I promise, just trust me. You do trust me, right?"

I closed my eyes and took a deep breath preparing for the pain. He kissed my forehead and pushed inside me quickly. Before I could scream, he silenced me with a kiss.

"Your body is mine, baby girl. Being the first

man to have you is such an honor," he groaned rubbing his thumb across my lips. "I will be the only man to touch you and fuck you." he whispered against my lips. He continued his soft slow thrusts until my hisses of pain turned into moans. When he was satisfied that my pain had subsided, his thrusts became deeper and rougher.

"Oh my...oh my." I moaned as my eyes rolled back. His thick shaft was coated in my juices as he shoved his length deep inside me again and again, harder and deeper each time. I noticed then that the gentleness that he showed me a few minutes ago was all that he possessed in bed. He was eager to claim me and take what he had chased all this time. My virginity was now his and no one would ever take that spot from him.

"You are mine; do you understand?" He growled pulling out of me and flipping me on my stomach.

"Yes," I moaned.

He chuckled, "get on all fours."

I did what I was told quickly, and he smirked. I missed the feeling of him inside me and he knew that. I gasped when he unexpectedly shoved himself back inside me. We moaned at the same time as I clenched around his massive shaft. I grabbed a fistful of the sheets when he found the spot that was going to send me over the edge.

"Looks like I found it."

"Vain please…don't stop please," I screamed grabbing the pillow. I was so close that my body started to tremble. His thrusts started to become sloppy and unsteady and that's when I knew that he was close as well. He grabbed a fist full of my hair and said my name as we both came at the same time. I screamed his name over and over again as I clenched around him. He leaned down and kissed me hard as I milked him dry. He closed his eyes and pulled out of me pulling me against his chest. We laid there not saying a word to each other. What was going to happen next?

Island Fun

I rolled over and smiled feeling Vain's warm body next to me. I could feel the ache between my legs, and I knew that last night really happened. I was no longer a virgin. I gave my virginity to the man lying next to me and I didn't know how to feel about it. I was shocked at myself because I didn't think that I would go through with it, but I did. I didn't know how I would feel after this and that is what scared me. I sighed and rolled over looking at his sleeping form. He was sexy even while he was sleeping. His long eyelashes rested on his cheek and his chest heaved up and down slowly. He looked innocent and sweet while he was sleeping. But I knew better, as soon as he opened his eyes, I would see the real Vain. I sat up slowly and kicked away the blanket. I grabbed my phone off the bedside table and cursed under my breath. Roman text me a few times and called me as well. I had twenty missed calls from him and that made me nervous. I read over his messages and smiled. He said that he was going to give me the two days that I needed. I was glad that he was giving me some space because I needed it. I ran my fingers through my hair, I needed to take a shower and get ready for the day. Now that it was officially daylight, Vain and I could go out and explore the island. I climbed out of bed and walked into the bathroom. I looked back to make sure that Vain was still sleeping and I smiled at him. Even though I had left the bed, he didn't move an inch. I closed the bathroom door silently and grabbed my toothbrush off the sink. I turned on my shower water and smiled feeling the water turn from cold to hot. When I was satisfied that it wasn't too hot, I stepped in and started to brush my teeth.

I wanted to talk to Roman, but I was still angry
with him. I knew that he would never do
anything to hurt me, but this hurt me. I hated
that I was in the dark about what happened
between him and my best friend. I rolled my
eyes if I should even call her that. The only
reason that she hung out with me was because
she wanted to be close to Roman. She never
cared about being my friend or being loyal to
me. I always accepted Tarma no matter what. I
accepted her when other people called her a slut
for sleeping around. I never judged her, and I
always told her to be careful if that is what she
wanted to do. I supported her and gave her a
great spot in my dance crew. It upset me that
she did that to me and still hid it. She didn't
even take ownership of what she did wrong
either. She just blamed the whole thing on my
brother. I grabbed the soap and started to wash
my body. I didn't want to spend the day
thinking about them because I knew that it
would upset me. The reason that I decided to
come with Vain to Spain was so that I could
getaway. I needed to get away for the weekend
and then return on Sunday and go to school
Monday. This would be a nice break away from
all the stress that was building up in my life. I

turned the shower water off and stepped out of the tub. I grabbed the big fluffy black towel and wrapped it around my body. When I walked into the bedroom Vain was sitting on the edge off the bed. He was on the phone, and I could tell that he was dealing with something important. I walked into the closet and tried to stay out of his way and business. If he was dealing with Mafia business than I wanted to be sure that he didn't think I was prying. My brother was still his enemy even though I was here with him.

"Ace, non ti preoccupare. I have this under control and if he continues…well, I'll kill him. I don't trust him or her so I will be keeping them close."

I frowned, who was he talking about. Although I went into the closet to put some distance between us, I still heard him. I stepped out of the closet and walked towards the bed slowly.

"Addio, I'll see you when I get home." He hung up the phone and sighed.

"What was that about?"

He turned to face me and shook his head. He stood up and walked past me towards the bathroom. "It's none of your concern." Before I could say another word, he closed the bathroom door behind him.

I couldn't help but feel angry that he acted that way towards me. We were supposed to be having fun together, but he was already in a bad mood. I rolled my eyes and grabbed my bikini putting it on. I wasn't going to let him ruin the day for me. I grabbed a fresh towel and slid on my sandals and walked downstairs. I wanted to go to the beach and when he was in a better mood, he could join me. I pulled open the front door and smiled stepping out of the house. This was going to be fun; I was sure of it.

I ran into the water and laughed feeling the cold-water splash against my skin. The waves were coming in and I kept trying to jump over them. The sun was shining, and the water was

cooling to my warm skin. I could see a
mountain-like view not too far from me and it
was beautiful. I kicked my feet up and smiled
floating on my back slowly. I just wanted to
relax and let the waves just carry me. It had
been a while since I had gone on a vacation.
The last vacation that we had was when I was
thirteen and we went to Bora Bora with my
parents. I loved it and I had a lot of fun. We
were talking about going back but then they
died. I shook my head and looked up at the sky.
The last thing I wanted to do was ruin the trip
by thinking about sad things. I looked down
and smiled when I saw the white sand beneath
my feet. I kept running my toes through it
because it felt good. The water was crystal
clear, so I was able to see the seafloor. This
beach was beautiful, and it was similar to Bora
Bora.

I walked back to shore and grabbed my towel. I
wanted to see what else the beach had to offer. I
could see food stands off in the distance and my
stomach jumped with joy. I was starving
because I didn't eat breakfast. Vain and I had
slept in, so when I woke up it was noon. As
much as I wanted to eat, I wanted to swim a

little more. So, I walked past the trucks and their tempting aroma. I smiled when a young child ran up to me and handed me an ice cream cone. He looked to be at least five years old. He ran away laughing and I watched him run back to a man. The man winked at me, and I waved at him mouthing the word thank you. From what I could see, everyone seemed so nice here. The only thing that made me sad was that I didn't speak Spanish. It would be a little difficult for me to have a conversation with most of the residents here. I licked the Vanilla ice cream and continued to walk towards the condo where I left Vain. I didn't think that I had been gone for that long. When I walked into the house Vain was standing there pacing back and forth.

He looked at me, "where the fuck have you been? I've been calling you and calling you and you haven't answered your phone."

I looked at him and frowned, "excuse me?" I don't know why he was talking to me like that, but I wasn't about to deal with this. I walked past him, and I could hear him following me.

"Athena, don't walk away from me when I'm talking to you." He grabbed my arm roughly and I yanked away from him.

"You won't talk to me like that. I went for a quick swim, and I came right back but I shouldn't have to explain that to you. Stop acting like you're my father Vain." I turned around and continued to walk towards the pool in the back of the condo. I tossed the ice cream cone into the trash and removed my towel and sandals. Before Vain could say another word to me, I dived into the pool. He was starting to piss me off and this was making me want nothing to do with him. When I came up for air he was standing by the stairs of the pool.

"Athena."

I turned to face him, "you won't take your anger out on me. Whatever Ace told you I don't care. I don't care that you're in a bad mood."

He smirked and quickly stripped down. I watched as he stepped into the pool and walked towards me. His eyes never left mine and I couldn't do anything but stand there frozen in place.

"The thing is…I'm in a bad mood but I know that you can make it better." He grabbed me and pulled me close to his body.

I cocked my head over to the side, "how do you figure that?"

He laughed untying the back of my bikini top. "I think you know."

He picked me up and wrapped my legs around his waist and I clung to him. He walked us over to the staircase and set me down. I looked up at him as he brushed his thumb across my bottom lip. I was confused about what he was doing when he grabbed the back of my head and guided me forward.

"I want you to suck it," he smirked.

I had never done it before, and I was scared because I didn't want to disappoint him. He applied pressure to the back of my head again and I opened my mouth allowing him to penetrate my mouth. He was so big that when he thrust forward, I gagged instantly. He groaned loudly and whispered my name. I wasn't sure what I was doing but I knew that I had to try. I took his shaft in one hand and stroked him slowly as I looked up at his hungry gaze. I traced my tongue up his length slowly and I watched as he hissed in pleasure and threw his head back. I teased him a little while longer until he growled and grabbed a fistful of my hair. Without giving him a warning, I took him into my mouth. I devoured him whole feeling him at the back of my throat. Again, this only made him more aggressive, and I could feel my throat expand every time he pushed his hips forward. He groaned loudly and pulled on my hair to stop me as he spilled his seed in my mouth. I moaned and smiled watching him pull his thick shaft out of my mouth.

"Swallow," he ordered out of breath.

Without hesitation, I swallowed every single drop and he smiled. He rubbed his thumb across my top and bottom lip quickly. I sat in silence smiling up at him. My mind was going crazy because I never thought that I would do that. He got down on his knees and licked his lips slowly.

"Now it's your turn," he chuckled untying my bikini bottom.

I want more

The weekend has been great and Vain, and I have done so much. I hated that tomorrow we would be leaving, and I would be returning home. I knew that I had to talk to my brother because I promised him. I looked down at my phone feeling it buzz in my hand. Roman sent me a text back and I smiled down at it.

4:36

R

Roman >

Text Message
Today 4:32 PM

Hey?

Hey

How are you ?

I'm good...how are you

Busy. Look I want to talk to you.
When you come home tomorrow
maybe we can go out for dinner

Yea That's cool with me

Ok

I love you

I love you too

Text Message

I walked down the street quickly. I was
shopping for something and Vain left the store
to take a phone call. He told me not to take too
long because we had dinner being delivered to
the condo. I finally found what I was looking
for five minutes after he left, and I was now
looking for him. I rounded a corner and sighed
when I didn't see him down the dark alleyway.
I didn't want to walk down there because I
wasn't familiar with this country, and I didn't
want to get lost.

I turned around and bumped into someone and I
quickly apologized. I was so clumsy, and I
wasn't watching where I was going. A man
laughed and I looked up to see him smiling
down at me. He was very handsome and tall.
He had a few tattoos that were visible to me.
His teeth were perfectly straight and white. His
hair was similar to Vain's because it was neat
and gelled back. Overall, he was a sexy devil,
but I knew that I shouldn't be checking him out.
He smiled at me again and I smiled back trying
not to be rude. He handed me the shopping bag
that I dropped, and I thanked him softly.

"Are you lost?"

I gulped and tried to catch my breath because he sounded so sexy. His voice was deep, and he had a heavy Spanish accent. I shook my head trying to pull myself together. "No, I mean um I kind of am. I'm looking for someone."

He smirked, "who?"

"His name is Vain Grey. Do you know him?"

He laughed, "yes. Who doesn't know him? His father Victor, is the king around here."

"I see, well that's who I'm looking for," I whispered tucking a strand of hair behind my ear.

He looked around before placing his hands in his pockets. "It's getting dark soon, how about I give you a ride?"

I shook my head slowly, "no. I don't think I should leave. I mean he just left me five minutes ago and I know he should be around here somewhere."

"I don't want to leave you alone. It gets dangerous in the city at night and a beautiful woman like you should not be walking around. I can take you home and you can tell him that you are heading home."

I was nervous to agree to get in the car with him because I didn't know him. I looked down at my phone and sighed. It was five o clock and the cars that were in the area started to leave. What other choice did I have?

"I won't hurt you, trust me." He smiled offering me his hand to shake. "I'm Antonio and you are?"

I took his hand and shook it, "Athena."

"Well, it's nice to meet you, Athena. My car is right over here," he turned around and walked towards a silver Mercedes. I followed behind him quickly and he pulled my door open for me before walking over to the driver's side. I climbed in and placed my bags on the floor by my feet and he started the car. I pulled my seat belt on, and he chuckled ignoring his. The engine came to life, and he took off driving down the street.

"Where are we going?"

I looked over at him, "um the condos near the beach. It's not right on the beach but it isn't too far."

He nodded his head, "I know what you're talking about. That's like a twenty-minute drive from here." His eyes didn't leave the road and I watched him carefully because I was still a little nervous.

My phone buzzed and I grabbed it out my purse. I looked down at the screen and the name that popped up was Vain. I opened the message and read it before replying.

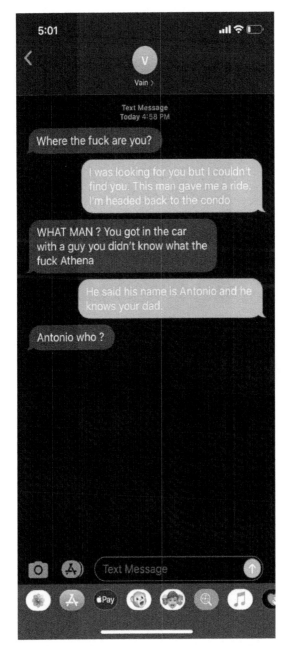

I knew that he would be upset but I didn't think
that he would be this upset. Before I could reply
to his text message, he started to call me.

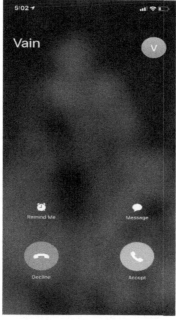

  I quickly pressed the end button because I
didn't want to hear him screaming at me in
front of Antonio. Right after denying him more
text messages came through.

5:04

V
Vain >

Text Message
Today 4:58 PM

Where the fuck are you?

I was looking for you but I couldn't find you. This man gave me a ride. I'm headed back to the condo

WHAT MAN ? You got in the car with a guy you didn't know what the fuck Athena

He said his name is Antonio and he knows your dad.

Antonio who ?

Why did you deny my call? Answer the fucking phone now

Don't play with me Athena

Vain calm down!!

Text Message

I texted him back quickly telling him to calm down. My phone lit up again and this time I answered it.

"WHAT THE FUCK!" I could hear him stop and go silent. "Where are you?"

"I told you that I was on my way back to the condo. I came out of the store, and I was looking for you, but you were nowhere to be found." I didn't get why he was so upset about me getting a ride home.

"Give him the phone."

I didn't hesitate to pass the phone to Antonio, and he took it. He placed the phone up to his ear, "Hello." He was silent for a minute before smirking, "I know, trust me I'll protect her. Look I'll have her home in about fifteen minutes. You can beat my ass when I get there." He laughed and hung up the phone. He handed it back to me and I took it placing it back in my purse.

"Don't worry about Vain, okay? He is just a big bully, but I'll handle him."

I looked at him shocked, "do you know him personally?"

"Yes, we are childhood friends. We grew up together here in Spain and then he moved to America. But he comes back to visit often though and so we get to meet up."

"Do you work for him?"

He laughed, "hell no. I work for his father. His

father lives here in Spain and he pays me more than Vain ever would. Don't tell him that I said that, he would kill me. I'm glad that I was the one who found you. If it were any other man, they would have been killed. Vain is very territorial and he has every right to be."

"Why is that?" I frowned.

"He had a girlfriend once and he really loved her. They met when he was nineteen and she was eighteen. He was going to marry her and everything. Long story short, on her twentieth birthday, she was kidnapped. As you know the mafia leader Satoni doesn't get along with Vain's family. So, just so he could hurt Vain and make him suffer they kidnapped the woman he cared most about. Satoni said that he would return the girl back unharmed if Victor paid him. Well, Vain's father refused to pay Satoni two million dollars to get her back. They gave Vain and his dad three days to come up with the money. Every day that went by and they didn't have the money, they would rape her and beat her. She was pregnant with Vain's child at the time all of this was going on. Vain found out because he was sent a video of them forcing her to take a pregnancy test and showing him, it was positive. So, after three days they killed her and sent her head to the family in a box. It was such a tragedy what happened to her." He looked over at me and smiled, "but you have nothing to worry about."

I couldn't believe what I was hearing. It was horrific and disgusting and I never knew that Vain had gone through something so terrible. I was starting to see the ugly side of the mafia and I didn't like it. I smiled weakly at Antonio and nodded my head slowly. I could see that he cared about Vain a lot and I was even more grateful that he was the one giving me a ride. Now I could see why Vain was so upset.

We arrived at the condo and Vain was standing outside pacing back and forth. I was cautious to get out of the car, but Antonio reassured me that it would be okay. I took a deep breath and climbed out of the car after Antonio. Vain ended the call he was on and stuffed his phone in his pocket.

"Ciao Amico," Antonio smiled pulling Vain into a hug.

Vain laughed and hugged him back, "Mio Amico…how are you?"

"I could say that I've been better. Your father has us working long hours these past few days. I hope it ends soon. How are you? How is America treating you?"

Vain shrugged, "I needed a break away from it. I work hard but it's nothing I can't handle. I would love for you to be my partner in New York."

Antonio smirked, "you know my home is here in Spain. But I'll think about it. Anyway, I have to go and don't be hard on her. She did deny me a few times, what can I say…I am very hard to tell no." He turned towards me, "Ciao Bellissima."

I waved at him, and he smiled climbing into his
car. I watched him speed away before turning
my attention to Vain. He grabbed his phone out
of his pocket, "go upstairs." That's all he said
before walking away and saying hey to the
other caller on his cellphone.

I took a deep breath and ran inside. I wanted to
get cleaned up and dressed for dinner before he
returned. I didn't want to make him any angrier
than he probably already was. I climbed the
steps quickly and raced into the bedroom to get
cleaned up and changed.

Vain walked into the room after keeping me
waiting for thirty minutes. He wasn't looking at
me at all he was texting on his phone. "Are you
ready for dinner?"

I didn't respond which caused him to look up at
me. I was sitting in the middle of the bed with
my hands in my lap. I looked up at him and
smiled cocking my head over to the side. "I
want more," I whispered running my finger

over my lace bra. When he left me in the store
to shop alone, I stumbled across this sexy
lingerie set. I never dressed up before and I
figured that it would be fun. The lingerie was a
beige bra with matching panties. The bra straps
had a line of rhinestones on them and the
padding that covered my breasts also had the
same line of rhinestones. The panties were
more of a thong. The straps of the panties had
the lines of rhinestones. It was sexy and I loved
it because the color looked nice with my skin
complexion.

He smirked and threw his phone on the chair
next to him. He walked towards the bed quickly
and I looked up at him. I licked my lips
watching as he pulled his shirt over his head
and dropped it at his feet. He cupped my chin
and brought his lips down to meet mine. I
moaned into his mouth pulling him closer to
me. I don't know where all this freakiness was
coming from, but I didn't care. He pulled away
running his hand along the top of my breasts,
"this is what you were shopping for?"

I nodded my head slowly and reached for his
belt. I wanted him now and I wouldn't take no

for an answer. He didn't stop me and that made me happy. I pulled his pants down and his erection sprang free. I didn't wait for him to tell me what to do this time. I quickly gripped his length and licked it slowly. He groaned in pleasure and grabbed a fistful of my hair. "Don't tease me," he growled.

I bit my lip and got on all fours so that he could get a good glimpse of my butt. Once I knew he was fully satisfied, I buried his thick shaft down my throat. I could hear him whisper my name and that turned me on. I pulled away and was about to continue to pleasure him, but he picked me up and threw me on the bed. I gasped when he grabbed my ankles and pulled me to the end of the bed. I could hear material ripping and I knew that he had ripped the lingerie.

"Vain, I just bought that."

He placed sloppy kisses on my inner thighs that made me arch my back. "So what?"

"Mm...what's for dinner?"

He looked into my eyes and smiled, "you." I moaned and clawed at the covers when I felt his mouth against my sensitive bud. He knew how to drive me crazy and now I was addicted.

Mistake

I rolled over and opened my eyes. The condo was quiet, and it was dark outside. I could hear Vain's soft breathing next to me and I smiled. I took a deep breath and stood up from the bed slowly. I was thirsty so I was going to go downstairs to get me something to drink. I walked towards the door and grabbed Vain's phone. It was midnight, I yawned and went to place the phone back down, but it vibrated in my hand. I instantly looked at it and saw that the name on the screen was Roxy. I frowned, what the hell did she want. There was a part of me that was telling me not to pry but another part of me was telling me to. I placed my thumb

197

on the button at the bottom and I was instantly denied access. His phone had a thumbprint as the verification code. I cursed under my breath and rolled my eyes when the phone started asking for a six-digit pin number. I pressed the sleep button and then I pressed it again and once again the phone was asking me for a thumbprint. I crept over to the bed silently and smiled when I saw Vain's hand hanging over the side of the bed. I grabbed his thumb gently and pressed it against the small button and the phone unlocked. I smirked and crept out of the room quickly. I walked into the guest bedroom and locked the door. Just in case he woke up he wouldn't be able to get in right away. I sat on the bed and my heart was pounding in my chest. Did I really want to go through his phone? I closed my eyes and took a deep breath. Yes, I needed to know the truth. I tapped on their text messages, and I was shocked by what I saw.

M

My Roxy ›

Text Message
Yesterday 10:22 AM

Daddy what are you doing ?????

You haven't been here in two days ! Where are you ?

I'm on a business trip. I'll be back Sunday

When you get back can we have some alone time 😔

You miss me huh

You know I do. I'm so wet for you. I miss you inside me baby

Don't tease me. You're making me hard just thinking about bending you over my desk.

Mmm that's what I want. Hurry up and come back daddy

I will be back Sunday.

Answer my FaceTime. I want you to see how wet I am for you.

Text Message

Don't tease me. You're making me hard just thinking about bending you over my desk.

Mmm that's what I want. Hurry up and come back daddy

I will be back Sunday.

Answer my FaceTime. I want you to see how wet I am for you.

Not now amore I told you that I'm busy but I'll call you later

Ok 😩

Yesterday 9:02 PM

Baby ?

You never called me back

Yesterday 11:55 PM

Really 🙄

No response ????????

Are you serious !??

Text Message

Tears came to my eyes after reading these text messages. He was talking to her the whole time that we were at the condo together. She was sending him pictures and videos, it was disgusting. Yesterday he was texting her while we were sitting down having breakfast together. He was such a lying piece of shit. I clutched my heart and cried softly. I don't even know why I was upset when I already knew what type of man he was. I wiped away my tears and grabbed the phone again. I wanted to know if there were any other women that he was talking to apart from me and Roxy. Right under her name, I found a girl named Tiffany. I clicked on their messages and started to read them silently.

I shook my head in disbelief, who the hell was she? I couldn't help but notice that he was texting her the same day he took me out to lunch. The same day that he took me out to lunch, he asked me to come to Spain with him. I didn't want to go any further because I knew that I was going to lose my mind. He was not different at all, the only reason that he took me to Spain is because he wanted to have sex with me. This is what he was good at. He was good at treating you well and being sweet and then he just moved on when he got what he wanted. That wasn't the case with these two girls though. He kept communicating with them even though he was here with me. I blamed myself for being so damn stupid. I was stupid to allow him to fool me like this. But he never fooled me. Sadly, I came here of my own free will and I said yes to him as well. I never asked him to be my boyfriend before I gave him my virginity. I just opened my legs to him as if it was nothing. I felt embarrassed, ashamed, and used and I blamed myself. I curled up on the bed and sobbed softly. I just needed some time alone because I knew that I would be heartbroken for a while.

I was packing my bag and Vain had woken up
and got in the shower. I woke up before he did
and replaced his phone before he noticed it was
gone. He said good morning to me, but I didn't
reply. I was upset with him and now the only
thing I wanted to do was to go home. I grabbed
my duffle bag and sighed placing it on the
floor. My stomach was growling, and I knew
that it was going to be a long ride home. I
walked downstairs to the kitchen to find
something to eat. I didn't waste any time
grabbing an apple off the dining room table and
taking a bite out of it as I walked into the
kitchen. I pulled the refrigerator open and
grabbed the orange juice and a glass out of the
cabinet. I poured me a glass and replaced the
orange juice. When I turned around Vain was
standing in front of the kitchen island with a
towel wrapped around his waist. He was staring
at me, and I pretended not to notice him. I
grabbed my phone out of my pocket and started

to scroll on Facebook.

He cleared his throat, "is something bothering you?"

I didn't answer him, I just continued to look down at my phone. I couldn't talk to him because I knew that I would explode. I was trying to be calm so that I could get home. That's the only thing that I wanted at this point anyway. I just wanted to go home and crawl into my bed and cry my eyes out.

"Athena, what the fuck is your problem? Are you going to ignore me or are you going to tell me what's wrong?"

I grabbed my phone and placed it in my back pocket. I looked up at him and he looked at me waiting patiently. I didn't give him the satisfaction of hearing me speak, I just walked right past him. I could hear him curse under his breath before following me up the stairs. What the hell did he want? Why couldn't he just leave me alone? I mean, if he didn't want to talk to me then I would leave him alone. I walked into the bedroom quickly. Before I could make it to the bed, he grabbed a fistful of my hair roughly. I closed my eyes and hissed in pain as he pulled me back against his body.

"You're not going to ignore me; do you understand me? What is your problem?"

"Vain, let go." That's the only thing that I wanted to say to him. I didn't feel like I owed him an explanation because he knew what he did. The only thing that he didn't know was that I was aware of the text messages that he had on his phone. I was going to tell him but why tell him what he already knew. He knew that he was texting them and entertaining them while he was here with me. He knew what he was doing, and he didn't care.

He threw me on the bed, and I looked up at him. He was pissed off and I didn't care. He was not about to bully me into giving in to him again. He grabbed my ankle and pulled me down to the edge of the bed. I tried to get away from him, but he quickly climbed on top of me. I pushed against his chest trying to stop him from going any further. He didn't pay attention to my weak attempts to stop him.

"Stop being this way, amore. I want you before we go," he whispered pressing his lips against my ear.

"Why don't you stop playing around and take me home so you can get back to your Roxy. She's wet and waiting for you back home," I smirked watching him pull away. I didn't mean to let the words slip past my lips, but they did.

He stared down at me and frowned, "how do you know that?"

"It doesn't matter, I know. I want to go home so please take me home. I don't want to be here any longer and I would like it if you got off of me."

He stood up quickly and walked into the bathroom slamming the door. Now he knew why I was upset and nothing else had to be explained. He knew that what he did was wrong, and I hope he felt guilty. I rolled my eyes, who the hell was I kidding? He didn't have a heart.

I walked inside my house and smiled when I saw Roman fixing dinner. He hadn't cooked in a long time, and I knew then that he was trying to make things right. I placed my bag by the door and walked into the kitchen to take a seat at the table. When Roman saw me he froze and just watched me. I knew that he was nervous, and he didn't want to say anything that would make me upset. I sighed and walked up to him wrapping my arms around him. I missed my brother, and I needed a hug right now. I was so stupid to allow one thing to change my life. I was mad at Roman and so I went to Spain and while I was out there, I only made more mistakes. I regretted leaving my home out of anger and making such a dumb ass decision. Roman hugged me back quickly and I couldn't help but sob uncontrollably. I was heartbroken and I felt like a piece of me was missing. I felt empty and hollow, I just didn't feel like myself anymore.

"What's wrong?" he whispered kissing the top of my head.

I shook my head, "I made a big mistake and now I feel so stupid. I know that I shouldn't have been so angry with you but I just...I don't know what happened."

He pulled away from me and frowned, "What mistake did you make? Athena, you're scaring me."

I took a deep breath and wiped away my tears, "Roman...you promise you won't be mad at me?"

He pulled me over to the table and pulled out a chair for me. He kneeled in front of me and placed his hands on my knees. "I'm your big brother and I'm here whenever you need me. I know the feeling of making mistakes, so whatever it is you can tell me. I know that we can get through it."

I looked into his eyes and debated with myself. Should I tell him what happened? Would he really forgive me, or would that cause more trouble for our family? I knew that Roman was the type of man to confront Vain. Could I really live with myself if that happened, and someone got hurt? I swallowed the words that I was going to say. "I ran away, and I broke the bracelet that you got me for my thirteenth birthday." I lied because I knew that I couldn't be honest with him, not right now.

He laughed, "is that it? You had me worried that it was something serious. I'll get you another one it's no problem."

I nodded my head and smiled, "okay."

"Where did you go?" He asked standing up and walking back over to the stove.

"I went to the beach. My friend has a condo, and we went there. I just needed some fresh air and some time to think." I licked my lips, "Roman...would you be mad at me if I had sex?"

He looked up at me in shock, "did you have sex?"

"No, I was just wondering if that would be something that would make you angry."

He walked over to the table and handed me my

plate. I thanked him softly watching him take his seat across from me. "Athena, I can't be upset with you about having sex. The only thing that I want is for you to be careful and I hope that you do talk to me about it. I know that it might seem uncomfortable, but I want to protect you. I don't want any man using you, you don't deserve that. The only thing I can do is be there for you when that time comes."

I smiled and grabbed his hand, "thank you."

He smirked, "I want to say that I'm sorry for not investing in your dreams. To make it up to you, here's a gift." He handed me a piece of paper and I took it from him slowly.

My heart felt like it dropped into my stomach. Was I seeing this correctly? In my hand, were two checks. There was one for Fifteen thousand dollars and one for twenty thousand dollars. "Roman…I…are you serious?"

He laughed, "yes. I want to start being fair to you and being open-minded."

I looked down at the checks and smiled. Things were finally looking up for me. Now I could pay Vain off and buy more stuff for my dance studio. I was no longer in debt to Vain and my life was back to normal.

Stalker

I didn't want to see Vain but yet I saw him. No matter how many times I tried to dodge him, he would appear. He wasn't getting the hint that I just wanted to be alone. I didn't want to talk to him, and I wish that he understood that. I tapped my finger on my notebook and rolled my eyes. The bell was taking forever to ring, and I was ready to go home. I wanted to take a long bubble bath and kick my feet up. I had a few shows that I had to catch up on. Inuyasha was getting better and better, and I had to see what happened next. I giggled and smiled

imaging myself at home in bed. I was so ready
to feel my soft cozy blanket. The teacher said
that there would be no homework tonight.
Hearing that made me even happier because
that was the last thing that I wanted to do. The
bell rang and I stood up and grabbed my bag.
We all exited the classroom quickly. I was
happy to know that I wasn't the only one who
was ready to get out of here. I pushed open the
front doors of the school and walked down the
steps. I could hear someone calling my name
and I looked up to see my crew. They were
waving me over and I laughed running over to
them.

"So, what's the plan for today?" Neji asked
putting his arm around me.

I laughed, "I told you guys that we don't have
practice today. So, go home and enjoy yourself
or do whatever makes you happy."

Eli clapped her hands, "ohhh I'm going to sleep
like a baby."

"How about you come home with me," Neji chuckled placing kisses on my cheek.

I smiled and turned to face him, "I would love to, but I have another date tonight. Inuyasha is calling me guys."

Neji smirked, "damn I've been beaten."

I shrugged, "you got to be quicker than that."

They laughed and I turned around waving goodbye to them. They walked the other direction together quickly. They all lived in the same area as each other. Unfortunately for me, I lived opposite of them. I used to be able to walk home with Tarma, but I didn't have her anymore. I sighed and looked up at the sky. Sometimes I missed her and sometimes I didn't. She really hurt me with what she did. Despite me being angry with Roman, he and I were working things out. He took me off curfew which was great. I needed the extra time to go and dance. I heard a car pull up next to me and I looked over to see Vain climbing out the car.

He walked up to me, and I turned to face him.

"WHAT THE HELL WAS THAT, HUH?"

I looked at him confused, what the hell was he talking about? "Vain."

"Don't fucking Vain me. Who the fuck is that guy who you were all over?"

I shook my head and turned to walk away. I refused to be talked to like this and I wasn't in the mood to be interrogated.

Before I could get a step away, I was yanked back by my hair. I struggled against him and that only seemed to piss him off. He pulled me against his body roughly, "don't walk away from me when I'm talking to you."

"GET YOUR DAMN HANDS OFF OF ME!" I gathered up all the strength I had, and I slapped him across the face. It seemed like everything stopped. He looked at me slowly and I gulped. My heart was pounding in my chest because I was afraid of what he would do. He licked his lip tasting the blood on the side of his lip. I knew that he was angry because he charged at me quickly. I tried to run but he caged me in his arms. I kicked and screamed trying to get people's attention when I realized that he was walking around his car. I wasn't going to allow him to put me in there. I bit his hand and he growled slamming me against the car roughly. I kept fighting against him until he slapped me across the face. It took me by surprise that he had hit me. He didn't allow me time to process it though because he opened the car door throwing me inside. I tried to open the door, but it wouldn't open. My cheek was stinging, and my head was spinning from the impact of his hand.

He climbed in the car and slammed his door. I tried to kick and scream but that really pissed him off further. He covered my mouth and took off driving so that he could get away from the area we were in. People were starting to come out of their houses, and I didn't think he wanted attention on him. Once we were far away from the school, he let me go and I moved far away from him. I knew that he was going to have to let me out the car and when he did, I was going to make a run for it. He pulled into an open field and turned to stare at me.

"Are you having sex with him?"

"Why does it matter to you?" I asked him, pressing my back against the door.

He chuckled, "because you belong to me. I would hate to break every bone in that boy's body for touching what belongs to me."

I looked at him with so much hate, "you don't own me. I'm not your property and you can't just show up demanding things. I don't owe you anything and I sure as hell don't owe you any answers. This is my life, and you are not my boyfriend."

He grabbed me by the throat, "I do own you. I remember telling you that only I could touch you. Do I have to refresh your memory?"

"Let me go," I whispered.

He let me go and sighed sitting back in his seat. "Athena, I don't like fighting with you."

"Go to hell," I interrupted him.

His jaw clenched and he licked his lips slowly. "Why are you being like this?"

"Because I want you to leave me alone. I don't want you stalking me and harassing me. You keep trying to force yourself into my life Vain."

He looked at me, "what changed? You were just in Spain begging me for more and now you don't want anything to do with me. What changed?"

"You have other women and I know that now."

He pulled me into his lap, and I looked away from him. "Look at me," he whispered cupping my cheek in the palm of his hand. "I love you, why can't you see that?" He kissed me roughly and I didn't push him away. "I love you, Athena. I can't stop thinking about you. You drive me crazy in the worst way."

I sobbed softly as he tried to wipe away my tears. I don't know why hearing him say that he loved me broke my heart more. Maybe that was because I had feelings for him. My feelings were deeper than what I tried to let him see. He started to place kisses all over my cheek and I closed my eyes tight. Why did I have to care about him? Although I fought with him, I felt complete when I was around him. The piece of me that was missing seemed to be there when I was near him.

He moved my hair over to the side and started to place soft kisses on my neck. "Amore, I miss you. I miss you so damn much, you don't understand. Don't lie to me because I know that you miss me too."

I bit my lip when I felt him slide my panties to the side. I could feel him rubbing himself against me and I couldn't help but moan softly. He closed his eyes and groaned reaching down undoing his pants. "Vain, I." A loud moan escaped my throat as he pushed himself deep inside me.

He held my hips and forced me to move up and down slowly. "You belong to me," he whispered against my lips.

Three days later

I tried my best not to think about Vain. We had sex in his car three days ago and I couldn't help but hate myself. I hated the fact that I gave in to him. I never meant to, but my body betrayed me. Not just that, I couldn't fight the fact that I did have feelings for him. I didn't want to act on those feelings because I knew that I couldn't. I hated the feelings that were deep in my body. I missed him when he wasn't around. I felt empty and lost and I craved him. I wanted him to be near me at all times. I wanted to feel his hands on my skin. It was driving me crazy and that was why I was forcing myself to stay away from him. He has been texting me and calling me these last few days, but I haven't answered. He left me roses in my dance studio and that resulted in me changing the locks on him. I went to buy my coffee at Starbucks this morning and magically my drink was paid for. I went to the mall with Eli yesterday and everything that I wanted to buy was already bought for me. I knew it was Vain and I didn't know why he was doing all this. He told me that he loved me, but I didn't know if that was true. He was horny at the time and so it could have just been said out of lust. I shook my head and continued to pack my things. I was doing another late night here at the studio. I grabbed my bag and turned the lights out. I opened the door and closed it locking it behind me. I heard footsteps and so I turned around and smiled expecting to see one of my crew members but to my surprise it was him.

"Athena."

I tried to walk around him, but he stopped me. I

wasn't in the mood to talk to him. I didn't want to.

"You changed the locks."

"Yes, you can't just walk in whenever you feel like it. I told you the other day that I just want to be alone Vain."

He looked around and stuffed his hands in his pocket. "Can we just talk?"

I sighed and unlocked the door letting him in. He walked in and smiled sitting down in the chair. I stepped in after him and locked the door since it was dark outside. I stood on the other side of the room watching him carefully.

"How are you?"

"I'm good...what about you?" I whispered.

He chuckled, "I miss you. I don't understand why you don't want to talk to me. I thought that we made things right a few days ago."

"Us having sex doesn't make things right. It

was a mistake having sex with you. I should have never done it. We can't keep doing this, okay? It is bad enough that I work for you. I can't get too caught up with you. It doesn't matter what I want or what you want. You and my brother are enemies, Vain."

He stood up and walked towards me slowly, "stop lying to yourself. You act like you don't like it when I touch you. You love it and instead of being honest about it you would rather make up excuses."

"It's not excuses," I interrupted him. I rubbed my forehead, "I told you already that I want to be left alone."

He cocked his head to the side, "really? How can you say that when I can tell that your body begs for me? You know it and I know it." He turned me towards the mirror and all I could do was go weak in his arms. I watched him undo his pants and his eyes never left mine. I didn't deny him when he pulled my skirt up and pushed my panties to the side.

"I want you to watch yourself. Look at yourself while I fuck you. Then you can tell me whether you want me to leave you alone or not."

I stared at my reflection and moaned when he buried his length deep inside me. I gripped the mirror and bit my lip roughly. I watched as his eyes never left mine. I couldn't shake the smile that was plastered on his face. He had won again, and he knew that.

He wrapped his hand around my throat pulling me to his body. I was a moaning mess as he reached down and placed his fingers in between my legs. "You are mine, all mine." He pushed me forward and I screamed his name as his thrusts became rougher and deeper.

Leave me alone

I sighed and relaxed in the hot water. This bath was just what I needed after a long day at my dance studio. My crew and I practiced all day to try and catch up on the past few dance practices that we missed. I was eager to get back in there and dance. The dance tournament was three weeks away and I wanted to be prepared. With the money that Roman gave me, I was able to go and get new outfits for me and the crew to dance in. It was going to be perfect, and I knew that when we danced again it was going to all come together. I closed my eyes and flipped through the shows that were on Hulu. I clicked on Siren and smiled laying my head back against the pillow I had in the tub. It has been two weeks since I lost my virginity. It has been four days since I last saw Vain. I didn't want to see him or talk to him. I missed work today and I didn't care because I was going to pay him off next Saturday anyway. He was going to be able to move on with his life and leave me alone. He got what he wanted and because I was so stupid, I gave in. I kept giving in to him and enough was enough. It was a learning lesson for me and despite everything that happened, I didn't hate him. I didn't blame him for being who he was. The only person that I blamed was myself. I've known him for a month, and he already got what he wanted. I rolled my eyes when I saw my phone vibrating. I grabbed it and shook my head. I looked at all the text messages that he was sending back-to-back.

Text Message
Today 4:24 PM

So you decided not to come to work ?

Stop acting like this and return my calls

It's been a week and i haven't heard from you

Get out of your feelings. It was just sex between us. Why are you upset ?

Answer my calls! Right the fuck now

Don't test me Athena

Alright you know what game on

Since you want to play...let's play

Text Message

His name popped up on my screen and I declined the call quickly.

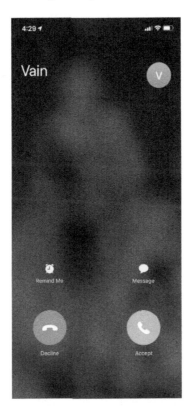

I sighed trying to finish reading the messages he sent. I didn't even get to finish reading the message because he called me again.

I declined the call and put my phone down on the table next to me. I didn't want to talk to him, why didn't he get the hint? He had called me twenty times today and I either ignored them or denied them. All I wanted to do was move on with my life and he was making that difficult. I sank lower in the tub and closed my eyes. I needed to go give him the check. It wouldn't be tomorrow though because that was my rest day. Monday was a school day so I wouldn't give it to him then. I was going to give him the check on Saturday or maybe Friday. That would give me a few more days to heal my broken heart.

I walked towards the Frozen Empire. It was a restaurant that served drinks. You could get food there as well and a lot of people hung out there. It was in the middle of the city, so anyone could go inside. It wasn't a part of the city that Roman or Vain owned. I was supposed to be meeting my dance crew here. Today was my relaxing day and this is what we did. I was trying to get back to being normal. I guess I called it normal because it was a life without Vain in it. I was learning to get back to doing what I was doing before my life was turned upside down. I giggled when I saw my crew waving at me from the window. The crew was a total of six members. Well, now we had five because Tarma was gone. The group was made up of two girls and three boys now that Tarma was gone. The only girl besides me was Eli. The three boys were Sam, Neji, and Jose. I walked into the restaurant and took my seat quickly.

"Hey, hey, hey." Jose laughed handing me a straw.

"I ordered your favorite," Eli said hugging me.

"Thank you so much," I laughed taking a long sip of my Guava black mango tea.

Neji chuckled and rubbed his hands together when the waitress brought our food. It smelled delightful and I was starving.

"We have barbeque wings, mango habanero wings, and smothered fries. "Is there anything else I can get for you?"

We all said no, and she walked away. I smiled and reached for a wing quickly. I wanted to catch up with the crew but first the food.

"Damn, you were hungry," Jose laughed.

"Mhmm," I smiled chewing the chicken in my mouth.

Eli cleared her throat, "I just want to say that I'm glad that Tarma is gone. She never wanted to help with anything, and she was dragging us down."

Jose nodded his head, "that's true. She never worked as hard as us and she was always hating on you. She tried to start this crazy rumor about you last week."

I rolled my eyes, "I know."

"We have to find a replacement for her though. As much as I agree with her being gone, we are uneven. The dance is going to be backward without her." Neji said stuffing some fries in his mouth.

"Maybe we just need to dance to a different song. I like the crew the way it is now," Eli smiled.

I shook my head, "I'm going to make sure that

everything is perfect. Trust me, we will win this." I smiled at each of them, and they smiled back. I knew that they would be worried, but they had nothing to worry about. I was going to make sure that we were ready in three weeks. We finished our food quicker than I expected and with all the talking we were doing I was shocked. It was time to pay and now they were debating on who was going to pay. I laughed and shook my head; they were such babies.

"I'll pay," I sighed. I waved the waitress over so that I could give her the money. "Hey, we are ready to pay."

She smiled at me, "your meal has already been paid for."

I frowned, "by who?"

She smirked, "I don't know him. He was sitting at the bar a few minutes ago. I guess he left." She turned and walked away, and I shrugged my shoulders. The crew got up and they walked towards the door, but I stopped.

"Come on Athena." Neji laughed putting his arm around my shoulder.

"I have to go to the bathroom; I'll text you when I get home." I smiled grabbing my jacket.

"Are you sure?" Eli asked worriedly.

I nodded my head, "yes. I'll see you guys' tomorrow at school." Neji placed a kiss on my cheek, and they left the restaurant. I looked down at my phone, it was eight-thirty. I walked towards the bathroom quickly. All that tea was finally making its way out of me. I pushed open the bathroom door and to my surprise it was empty. I found a stall and quickly emptied my bladder. Once I was done, I walked out of the stall and washed my hands. I opened the bathroom door and headed towards the front door to leave but I spotted Vain sitting at a table near the door. He was surrounded by a few guys and three girls. One of the guys was Ace, the other men and women I didn't know. My heart was pounding in my chest because I didn't want to see him. I closed my eyes and gathered up the courage to continue to walk towards the door. I looked down at my phone trying to make it seem like I was busy. I mean what girl didn't do that? I made it to the door, and I pushed it open feeling grateful that I made it out. I turned around to look back into the restaurant. My heart felt like it froze in my chest because Vain was staring right at me. I didn't waste any time turning around and running down the street. I wanted to get far away from him as possible.

"Excuse me…sorry…excuse me," I tried to dodge people, but they were in my way. I looked over my shoulder and smiled when I realized that he wasn't following me. I tucked a strand of hair behind my ear and continued to walk home. As I walked down the street, the streets lights began to come on. I didn't live too far from the restaurant. I could have called a driver, but I didn't feel like I needed one. I took a deep breath and closed my eyes picking up my pace. The sooner I got home the better.

I walked into my house and smiled flicking on the lights. I called out to my brother but no answer. He was going to probably have a late night tonight. I grabbed my phone and sent him a text letting him know that I made it home safely. I checked the clock, and it was Eight-fifty p.m. It wasn't too late, but it was time for me to take a shower and climb in bed. I made sure that all the doors were locked, and I ran upstairs to my room. I undressed and grabbed a towel wrapping it around myself. I went into the bathroom to brush my teeth and start my shower water. I forgot to get extra clothes to sleep in and so I walked back into my room.

"You have a lovely home."

I looked up quickly and there sitting on my bed was the devil himself. So many thoughts were running through my head. How the hell did he get in my house? When did he get here? How did he get here? I stepped back when he stood up. I was trying to get as close to the bathroom as possible. My plan was to run in there and lock the door. My phone was in there and I would be able to call the police.

He smirked, "you have nothing to say?"

"Vain, get out. You have no right to come into my home. You have no right to stalk me, I'm not your property." I turned around and tried to run but before I could reach the bathroom, I was yanked by my hair roughly.

"You are such an ungrateful bitch. I took you to Spain and spoiled you the whole time there. I bought that Condo for sixty thousand dollars for you. I let you spend one thousand dollars on clothes for yourself. I told you that I loved you. You get angry about some text messages on my phone and ignore me. You ignore me after everything that I've done for you, really?"

I struggled against him, "stop. I'm warning you that I will call the police on you. I want you to leave right now."

He slammed me against the wall, "Is that so? Is that what we are resorting to?" He wrapped his hand around my throat, "call them." He stepped back and smiled at me. "Go ahead and call them because by the time you end the call with them...I'll make you regret it."

We stood there staring at each other for a while. I wanted to move but my body was frozen in place. I was shocked and most of all scared. "How did you get in here?"

"I thought you were going to call the police on me?" He smirked laying down on my bed.

I stepped closer to him, "I'm not joking. How did you get in my house?"

He shrugged and pulled out his phone, "why does it matter?"

"Why are you here? What do you want?"

"I want to know why you missed work and why you have been ignoring my calls?"

He had to be kidding me, right? He knew why I was ignoring him and now he was acting clueless. I knew that I didn't want to go over the same stuff that we kind of talked about in Spain and so I decided to lie.

"My monthly cycle came, and I haven't been feeling good. Besides, my body has been sore."

He frowned, "why come you didn't tell me?"

"Because I don't feel like I should have to tell you when I'm bleeding. Somethings I would like to keep to myself." I folded my arms across my chest and stared at him.

He sighed, "I don't like being ignored. I tend to act a little crazy but I'm not sorry for it."

"I can tell because you have been stalking me."

He sat up quickly, "stalking…is that what you call it?"

I smirked, "what do you call it?"

He stood up and walked over to me slowly. "I call it keeping an eye on what belongs to me."

I put my hand on his chest to stop him, "I don't belong to you. You took my virginity, so what? You better be happy that you got that at least. Now that you got what you want you can leave me alone."

He cupped my chin forcing me to look at him, "Is that what you truly want?"

I nodded my head quickly, "yes." It was no secret that I wanted to be left alone. I didn't want anything to do with Vain. Yes, we had a good time, but that time was over. The time ended with him claiming my virginity but that wasn't something I could stress about. I wanted things to end before I got too attached to him.

"I'll give you what you want, but don't forget that you're still on a contract with me." He kissed my forehead and smiled, "you get to see what it's like when I don't care about you."

"You need to leave," I whispered.

"Say no more, Athena. See you Saturday…goodnight." He chuckled walking out of my bedroom.

I stood there with my hand on my heart and tears in my eyes. Once I heard the front door open and close, I ran downstairs to lock the door. I was glad that he was gone because I could finally cry in peace. These past few days I've been trying to act so strong, but the truth was…

I had fallen in love with Vain.

$Paid Off$

I pulled open the door to the club and stepped inside. I was here to pay off Vain finally. I looked around but to my surprise, I didn't see anyone here. It was two o clock, and the doors were unlocked so I knew someone had to be here. I placed my hand in my pocket to make sure that the check was still there. I was nervous because I didn't know what to expect. Vain hasn't been calling or texting me. The last time that I saw him was the night he was at my house. He told me that he would leave me alone and surprisingly he has. Now we wouldn't have to worry about each other for good because I had the money to pay him off. I walked towards the steps and started to take them one at a time.

My heart was pounding in my chest and my hands were trembling.

"Hey, where you headed to?"

I turned around to see Ace standing at the bottom of the stairs. I looked back up towards the stairs before turning to face him. "Oh, I was looking for Vain. If he is busy, I can come back later."

He smirked, "no he isn't busy. I'll walk you up there." He climbed the steps quickly and I followed behind him.

Ace and I haven't talked since we met. Being around him made me think of Tarma and it bothered me. He was the reason that the truth finally came out. Even though I lost her as a friend, I got the money to pay off Vain. I've been wanting to text her, but she hasn't text me so I'm leaving her alone. I don't know if we would ever talk but I had to put that behind me for now.

Ace looked over his shoulder, "have you talked to Tarma?"

I looked at him shocked, "no. Why?"

He laughed, "she was fun. I miss her and she disappeared out of the blue. I've been calling and texting her but no answer."

"You should know that you are the reason that she had to go to California. If you weren't having sex with her without a condom, she would be here."

He raised an eyebrow, "it was her idea to not use a condom. If she told you that it was me, you're wrong." He turned to face me, and I rolled my eyes. I didn't care what he had to say. He was just like every other guy. "Here you are," he knocked on the door and left me standing there alone.

Vain yelled come in and I walked inside quickly. To my surprise, all the girls were in there with him. They turned to look at me and I frowned. What the hell was going on?

"Glad you made it, baby doll. Unfortunately, you are an hour late for the group meeting." He looked at me from his desk and I gulped.

"W-what group meeting? I wasn't told that we were having a meeting." He had to be kidding me, right? I had no idea that we were having a meeting.

He grabbed his phone and looked down at it, "I sent you a text. You chose to ignore it and that has nothing to do with me. Now the meeting is over, and I don't intend on repeating myself, so hopefully one of the girls will catch you up."

Roxy smirked and stood up, "we discussed jobs. We all chose new jobs to do and since you weren't here, it was chosen for you. You will clean the club before, during, and after our shifts. You will need to make sure to come in at seven on Saturdays and clean. The club should be clean by three in the morning because that is when Vain leaves. If it is not clean, you will come in on Sunday and finish. It is also your job to clean the back rooms and bathrooms. You will also still serve drinks as well. Do you understand?"

I frowned and shook my head, "okay." I don't know why he was acting this way, but it was pissing me off. I never got a text message about a meeting and because of that, he was acting like a jerk. He was going to make me clean the club and stay an extra hour after everyone left. What type of treatment was that? The other girls looked at Vain and he smiled. I wanted to slap him because he was doing this on purpose. I wasn't stupid and I knew that he was trying to punish me for rejecting him. I held my head up high and took a deep breath. I wasn't about to show him that he got to me. Especially since I was about to pay him off. The joke was on him, and I couldn't wait to see his face.

"Okay, go get ready ladies."

They stood up and walked out quickly. I didn't follow them because I had to talk to him. Roxy seemed a little irritated that I was staying behind, but I didn't care. She slammed the door behind her, and I rolled my eyes. I stepped closer to his desk, and he didn't budge from looking at his phone.

I cleared my throat, "Vain."

"What do you want? I thought I told you to go get ready. Why are you still standing here?"

I pulled the check out of my pocket and slid it on his desk. He looked up and frowned and I smirked. "Sorry, but I won't be working tonight. You have been paid off." I turned to leave because there was nothing more for us to talk about.

"What is this?" He asked sitting back in his chair.

"It's a check. I don't have to work for you anymore. So, you can find someone else to clean the club for you."

He chuckled, "you think it is that easy?"

"It doesn't matter if it's easy or not. You have your money and now I am out of your contract." What part of it wasn't he getting? I paid him off so now he could leave me alone. Why was he acting like the check wasn't good enough?

"Listen, Amore, you signed a contract me. In that contract, it says that you have to work for me for six months. You can't just bring me a check and think it is good enough." He threw the check at me and stood up, "like I said before…go get ready."

I shook my head in disbelief, "fuck you." I turned around and headed towards the door. I wasn't going to listen to him. He couldn't do this, and I wasn't about to allow him to.

Before I could place my hand on the doorknob, I was pulled back roughly by my hair. Vain pulled me over to the couch and grabbed my waist pulling me down into his lap. "Do I have to fuck you in front of your brother? Is that what it will take to prove that you are mine?"

I froze in place when I heard him say that. Would he really go that far to keep me here? I turned around to face him, "so you would blackmail me?"

He smirked, "now it seems that I have your attention. Like I said before, you can't just bring me a check and expect my contract to be voided. It's not blackmail, Athena. You signed a contract with me and it's over when I say that it's over."

I struggled against him trying to break free. "I don't belong to you, I'm not your fucking property."

He raised an eyebrow, "no? Do you want to put your answer to the test? Just like I got in your home, I can do much more. You know that, so why are you testing me?"

"Because I don't have to deal with you. You're doing all this because I won't be with you. I don't have to be with you if I don't want to. And now you're going to blackmail me because I finally got the money to get away from you."

He laughed, "I didn't want you, Athena. The only thing I wanted was to fuck you and I did just that. I will continue to do that because you know you love it. You love me and that is why you are so desperate to pay me off. Now, stop wasting my time and go get dressed before I bend you over my desk."

"Fuck you, I'm not working for you," I cut him off before he could go any further.

He smiled and grabbed my arm roughly pulling me towards the door. "Fine by me. I don't mind showing your brother how much you love his enemy."

I struggled against him, "NO. PLEASE VAIN DON'T!"

He stopped and cupped my chin forcing me to look at him, "what did you say?"

I couldn't help the sadness that washed over me. I couldn't help the feeling that occurred in my chest. I felt defeated and broken-hearted. I knew that Vain was ruthless, but I never thought that he would become this way. He never acted this way before and it bothered me. Tears slid down my cheeks and I was shocked when he didn't comfort me. He just stared at me as I sobbed softly. "I'll finish the six months with you," I whispered.

He let me go, "get out."

I didn't wait to be told twice. I ran out of his office and slumped down into the hallway sobbing. How could I complete six months with him? I didn't want to be here, and I didn't want to work for him. I wiped away my tears and frowned. There was only one way to beat him at his own game. I hated to have to do it, but I knew that it was probably my only way. Maybe if I seduced him and promised him that I would be his, then maybe he would let me go. I stood up and bit my lip. It was something that I was willing to try.

I knocked on Vain's office door. My shift was over, and I finished cleaning the club. It wasn't that messy today which was great. I heard him say come in and I walked in quickly. He was standing by his bar fixing himself a drink. I took a deep breath and walked towards him. I wasn't sure what I was doing but I had to do something to get on his good side. I didn't change out of my attire from earlier. Maybe seeing me like this would turn him on.

"I'm finished," I whispered.

He turned to face me gulping down his drink. "Okay, go home."

I stepped closer to him, and he watched me carefully. "I was hoping that maybe we could talk. I hate when we fight," I looked down at my heels.

He shrugged, "what do you want to talk about?
You know that I'm a busy man."

I closed my eyes and contemplated giving up
because he was being rude. I could tell that he
wasn't in the mood, and I didn't want to push
him further. A small voice in me told me to
continue despite the feeling in the air. I had to
seduce him, that was the goal. I wouldn't give
up and run away, not this time.

I walked up to him and placed my hand on his
chest. I wasn't sure what I was doing but I had
to go with it. "Are you too busy for me?"

He looked at me and smirked, "ah I see." He
stepped towards and me I stepped back the
closer he got.

"See what?" I whispered looking up at him.

He grabbed me and lifted me onto his desk
quickly. I gasped and clung to him hearing him
laugh. He parted my legs and stood between
them trailing his hand down my back.

"You miss me already, huh?"

I nodded my head slowly, "yes. I want to be yours."

He started to place kisses on my neck, and I closed my eyes and moaned. "You want to be mine but why?" He asked in between kisses.

I didn't answer him, instead, I grabbed his belt and undid it. He watched me and I smiled at him. I knew that his mind was going crazy and that is exactly what I wanted. I licked my lips slowly sliding my panties to the side. I could see the lust swimming in his eyes and that turned me on. I was glad to know that I was turning him on as well. He yanked his pants down and grabbed my legs yanking me forward. He was eager to penetrate me, but I stopped him.

"Promise me that you will take the check."

He grabbed me by the throat and slowly began to enter me. "Fuck," he whispered against my lips.

"Vain," I moaned.

He smiled, "Hai provato…no scusa." He started to thrust into me roughly, "You are mine, all mine."

Graduation

It has been a month and I'm still working at the club with Vain. I have to stay late after everyone leaves to clean. I've been exhausted trying to keep up with that and school. I would say dance practice but our season is over. Our practice starts in August, and it ends in May. Once we compete in the dance tournament, we take a break. Speaking of the dance tournament, we danced last week. We did better than the group thought we did, and we came out in second place. I was heartbroken because I thought that we would get first place this year.

Overall, it wasn't too bad because we still walked away with something. The second-place prize was twenty-five thousand dollars. We split that between the five of us and we all got five thousand each. This was going to be our last time dancing together because we were graduating from high school. The other crew members would be going off to college. Eli got accepted into Bayside University. She was excited to start her journey to become a doctor. Her mother was an alcoholic and she would never acknowledge Eli. Since the age of six, her grandmother has had to raise her. Her father died when she was a baby, and she never knew him. Neji got accepted into Full Sail performing arts college. It was located in Chicago, which was not too far away. He wanted to continue his dancing career because he wanted to become famous. Neji lived in a two-parent household, and he had a younger sister named Dion. His parents were lawyers who represented all kinds of celebrity's and they put their all into their children. Sam got accepted into Full Sail performing arts college as well. He had the same goal as Neji, and they were excited to go together. Sam lived with his mom; his dad walked out on them years ago. His mother worked at a local grocery store, and she tried to provide for her children as best as she could. Sam has a younger sister named Kelly and he has a younger brother named Kyle. Due to his mother struggling to make ends meet, he wasn't sure that he would be able to go. But Neji's parents reassured his mom that they would take care of everything. Jose was accepted into The University of Texas. He was following in his parent's footsteps by becoming a marine biologist. His parents were big marine Biologists and they studied marine animals all over the world. They spent most of their time traveling than at home these days. Jose has no siblings, and he was happy about that. Then there's me, I got accepted into Full Sail performing arts college with Neji and Sam. I didn't tell Roman yet because I know that he will be upset. My life is with the mafia, and he didn't want me to forget that.

On another note, today is graduation day and I can't help but feel nervous. I felt like I would throw up any moment. The arena was filled with people, and I couldn't think straight. There were five people in front of me and I hated that. I wanted it to be one hundred people in front of me. I didn't want to trip and fall. The stage looked so long until I reached the principle. I closed my eyes and took a deep breath trying to force myself to calm down. Neji was standing in front of me, and I shook my head. I knew that he was itching to tease me, and I was not in the mood.

"Calm down Athena, you'll be fine."

I nodded my head and took another deep breath. He was right, I needed to calm down. It wasn't that big of a deal anyway. I walk across the stage and shake the principle's hand, then take my diploma. Simple…right? They called Neji's name, and he walked away leaving me in the front of the line. I was so happy to see him wave at the crowd and enjoy himself. He took his diploma and stopped for a picture before walking off the stage.

"ATHENA VINTALLI."

I heard my name, and I took off walking. I smiled and looked down at my feet hearing Eli screaming. Everyone was clapping and I was grateful that I got the same love as Neji. I shook the principles hand and grabbed my diploma.

He congratulated me and I thanked him. I looked at the camera and smiled before walking off the stage. That wasn't so bad after all.

I hugged Roman tight, and he laughed rocking me from side to side. After we all exited the arena, he was waiting for me. He had a big bouquet of flowers with him, and it brought tears to my eyes. My brother could be sweet when he wanted to be.

He handed me the flowers, "you look beautiful."

I giggled, "you act like you didn't see me before the ceremony. You drove me here remember?"

"I know, I didn't get the opportunity to tell you that. I also wanted to tell you that I'm very proud of you. You've worked so hard, and it shows with you standing here in your cap and gown." He grabbed my hand and squeezed it.

"Thank you, I'm looking forward to what I will do next."

He smiled, "I know you're going to be mad at me. I can't have dinner with you tonight, but I will tomorrow."

I frowned at him and sighed, "why?"

"Mafia business, you know how that goes. I have to fly out to Chicago tonight. You know that I would never leave you hanging if it wasn't important."

I looked down at my feet, "can't you just get out of the mafia and live a normal life? Why do we have to live like this? Dad wanted this but mom didn't." I didn't understand my brother. He didn't have to pick up the business after our father died. Everything that my parents owned was paid off and given to us when they died. They had one million dollars in a bank account for us.

He shook his head, "you need to understand that money doesn't stop. What we need, doesn't stop. You think that one million dollars is a lot of money but that is all they left us. It is two of

us and that money has already been split down
the middle. You have five hundred thousand
dollars and I have five hundred thousand
dollars. Your money is in a bank account that
you can't touch until you're eighteen. You are
getting older, and we can't live together
forever. I have to buy my own house and start
my own life. You say that you want me to live a
normal life but I'm the son of a mafia leader."

"Why work so hard if we are not as rich as the
other leaders? We don't make nearly as much
as the other families do." I didn't understand
him at all. He acted like risking his life was
worth the money that he got.

"I don't care what these other families make. I
make thirty thousand dollars a day. I work
seven days a week, so that means in a week,
I'm bringing home two hundred and ten
thousand dollars. In a month, I'm bringing
home eight hundred and forty thousand dollars.
In a year, three million dollars. I don't have to
count the little extra hundreds in that three
million. It shouldn't matter," he paused and
rubbed his head. "You know what, I'm done
with this conversation. Benny will take you

home, okay?"

He walked away leaving me standing alone and I couldn't help but feel sad. I could tell that I hurt his feelings and I didn't mean to do that. I had no idea that Roman was bringing home three million dollars a year. I was so damn stupid to insult him like that. What the hell was I thinking?

I looked up and frowned when I saw Vain standing right in front of me. My heart was pounding in my chest because what if people saw us? I grabbed his arm and pulled him around the back of the building quickly. We hadn't spoken to each other in weeks, and I was grateful. I did my job, and I went home, which was fine. I would see him talking to other women and flirting with them, but I didn't care. I was done with him but here he was again. I knew that this was all a game for him, and I was done playing.

"You look beautiful, baby doll." He cupped my chin forcing me to look at him.

I yanked away from him, "you can't be here.

Why are you here?" I looked around trying to make sure that no one was watching me.

He smirked and bit his lip, "I was coming to congratulate you. You are becoming a woman now, you're not a little girl anymore."

"Well thanks," I mumbled trying to walk away from him.

He grabbed my arm to stop me, "how about I take you out for dinner?"

I shook my head, "nope. I'm fine, I was heading home anyway."

He sighed leaning his back against the building. "Athena, come to dinner with me. It would be a nice way to show that we are still friends. I don't want a bad relationship with you. We can go wherever you want to go, and it doesn't have to be for long.

I turned around to face him, "fine. I will go to dinner with you but that is it. I don't mind being your friend."

He smiled, "great. The car is right over there."

I followed him quickly. I didn't like fighting
with Vain either, but he made it hard. I was
second-guessing my decision to go to dinner
with him, but it was too late. As long as we had
dinner and that was all, I was fine with that. He
opened the car door for me, and I climbed in.
He walked over to his side and got in. I looked
over at him and he smiled at me. I didn't return
the smile, I turned to stare out the window.

Dinner was great and now I was headed back
home. I was exhausted and I was ready to climb
into my warm cozy bed. Roman wouldn't be
home tonight, so I would be there by myself. I
didn't mind spending some time alone anyway.
I had to think about how to tell my brother that
I was going off to college. I knew that he would
give me a hard time, but he couldn't control me
forever. I frowned when I noticed Vain pulling
into his driveway. What the hell were we doing
here?

"Vain, I told you that I wanted to go home."

He shrugged and climbed out of the car, "come on. We can have a drink and then I will take you home."

I rolled my eyes and climbed out of the car slowly. My feet were aching due to wearing heels all day. I didn't feel like being bothered with his bullshit tonight. I knew that if I gave him a hard time, he would give me one. He opened the door and I walked into the house. He closed and locked the door behind me, and I took that as an opportunity to take my shoes off. He walked past me, and I followed him. He tried to make small talk, but I wasn't really in the mood. I was very sleepy for some reason, and I wanted to lay down. We walked into his bedroom, and I didn't waste any time climbing into his bed.

He chuckled, "are you tired?"

"Mhm," I mumbled with my eyes closed. It was only eleven o clock, but I felt like I pulled an all-nighter. My body was weak, and sleep was calling out to me. I frowned when I felt soft kisses being pressed on my neck. I knew that it was vain, but I wasn't in the mood.

"Vain…no," I whispered pushing against his chest weakly. I didn't feel like myself at all which was strange. I was too tired to even open my eyes.

He grabbed the strap of my dress and pulled it down. "Why? I miss you and I know that you miss me."

"Vain," his mouth quickly covered mine before I could say anything else.

"I want you," he whispered against my lips. He slid my dress up and spread my legs. I opened my eyes and looked down at him and he smiled at. He slid my panties down my legs quickly. I bit my lip waiting for him to bury his face between my legs. He didn't tease me like I thought he would, he hooked my leg over his shoulder and disappeared between my legs.

Vain POV

I groaned and woke up climbing out of the bed.
I glanced at the clock on the wall and groaned
again. It was two in the morning, and I didn't
remember passing out. I looked over to see
Athena sleeping peacefully beside me. She was
naked and I smiled remembering the love that
we made a few hours ago. She kept telling me
no until she couldn't anymore. I placed the
blanket over her naked body and climbed out of
bed. I stood up and stretched grabbing my
phone off the nightstand. I saw a text message
from an unknown number. I opened the text
and stared at it already knowing what was
going on.

6:24

U

Unknown >

Text Message
Yesterday 10:58 PM

Lui sta guardando

stai attento con la tua piccola bellezza

Text Message

"Fuck," I whispered.

Pregnant

Two Weeks Later

I hadn't talked to Vain in two weeks and every time that I called him, he wouldn't answer. I would text him, but he wouldn't respond. The last time that I saw him was on my graduation day. He took me to his house, and I fell asleep, but I woke up naked in his bed the next day. I knew that we had sex and we had sex again before he took me home. I tried to talk to him while we were at work, but he did everything he could to dodge me. He ignored me when I went into his office which caused me to leave. I don't know why he was doing that all of a sudden. Maybe I didn't want to accept the fact that he used me. He wanted a quick one-night stand and he got it. I was so damn stupid to go with him that night. Once again, he won, and I lost. I was mad at myself because I knew that I couldn't be mad at him. I sat down on my bed and stared out the window. I couldn't sleep for the past three nights. I needed to talk to Vain because I think that I might be pregnant. My monthly cycle hadn't come, and I was three days late. I was never late, and I was scared because I couldn't be pregnant. Roman would kill me and once he discovered by who, there was no telling what he would do. I picked up my phone and decided to text Vain again. I needed to talk to him about this.

I smiled down at the phone and took a deep
breath. He decided to meet me which was great.
I stood up from my bed and placed my phone in
my pocket. I needed to leave now, that way I
could be on time. The last thing I wanted to do
was keep him waiting. I ran down the steps and
smiled at Roman. He didn't pay me much
attention and I didn't have time to reason with
him. I would apologize tonight over dinner. I
opened the front door and stepped out into the
hot summer weather. This was going to be a
scary conversation.

I stood by the lake and waited patiently for
Vain to show up. I had been waiting for ten
minutes and I was starting to think that he
wouldn't come. I shielded my eyes from the
blazing sun and sighed. I wanted to take a
pregnancy test, but I didn't want to take it
alone. Now I see what Tarma was feeling when
she went through this. Luckily for her, she had

me. I wanted to cry because I didn't want to be pregnant, not right now at least. I was so stupid to be reckless with Vain and he knew that I wasn't on birth control. He never wanted to use a condom, but I never pressured him to.

"What did you want to talk about?"

I heard him speak and my heart felt like it was melting down to my stomach. I didn't think that he would come but I'm glad that he did. He looked sexy today in his white t-shirt and black jeans. I cleared my throat turning my attention back to the water.

"Thank you for meeting with me," I whispered.

"You have five minutes, so spit it out, Athena."

I frowned; I wasn't used to him acting this way towards me. I guess he really didn't want anything to do with me. That showed me further that he wouldn't take this news well. He would be upset, and I didn't feel like dealing with it. I swallowed the lump in my throat turning to face him. "It doesn't matter, um don't worry about it. I…I um…it's nothing."

I couldn't fight the tears that slid down my cheeks. I was hurting and he didn't care. I needed to talk to him, but he didn't care. He didn't care about me, and it showed right here and now. He was being honest when he said that he was just having sex with me.

I tried to walk away but he grabbed my arm, "what's wrong?"

"Vain I…I think that I'm pregnant."

He let go of me and frowned. I could see the anger in his eyes, "what the fuck do you mean?"

I stepped towards him, but he stepped back, "I wanted to."

"Don't give me that bullshit," he cut me off. "You're not going to scream pregnancy to try and keep me."

I stared at him confused, "I'm telling you the truth. I have no reason to lie to you and I would never try and trap you. I wanted to use a condom, you didn't. The only reason that I suspected I was pregnant is because I'm late."

He ran his fingers through his hair and cursed under his breath. "How late?"

"Three days," I whispered.

He looked at me, "has this been confirmed? Have you taken a test or been to the doctor?"

I shook my head, "I wanted to talk to you first."

He sighed, "get in the car. I'll take you to get a test. You can take it at my house. We need to know if you're pregnant or not. Playing the guessing game won't help either one of us."

I climbed into the car, "What if I am...what will we do?"

He looked at me, "you won't like my answer. Let's just hope that you're not," he started the car and took off driving.

My heart was pounding in my chest. I had taken two tests and I was waiting on the results from them. I didn't want to be pregnant and Vain didn't want me to be pregnant. I was scared and I couldn't think straight. He had given me some water, but I couldn't get it down. I felt like I was going to throw up waiting for my results. Vain stood up and walked into the bathroom to get the tests. My body was shaking all over and I couldn't stop it. He walked out of the bathroom carrying the two tests and I stood up slowly.

"Negative," he said handing them to me.

I placed my hand on my heart and looked down at them. I was so grateful to see the negative sign on them. "Thank god," I smiled clutching them to my chest.

"I have a doctor here to do a blood test. I want to make sure that the tests are telling the truth."

I was nervous about that because I didn't like needles, but I knew that I had to go through it. I followed him into the kitchen and a woman smiled at me. She was African American, and she was beautiful. Her curly black hair touched her middle back, and she was petite in size.

"Hello, my name is Dr. Jewels, and I will be taking a sample of blood from you. Take a seat right here please."

I walked over to the stool and sat down next to her. Once again, my heart was pounding in my chest because what if my blood tested positive? She grabbed my hand and squeezed it tightly. I knew that she was trying to reassure me that I would be okay.

"I will take a small quick sample. You will know the results in five minutes. It will be painless, I promise."

She grabbed my arm and rubbed a cold alcohol pad in the center. She grabbed the needle, and I moved my arm away from her.

She smiled, "don't look while I'm doing this, okay?"

"Okay," I whispered.

"I heard you just graduated, that must be exciting, right?"

I smiled, "yes. I hated school so I'm happy that I'm free from it."

"I understand that. I didn't favor school much myself." She giggled and stood up, "all done."

I looked down at my arm and rubbed the small band-aid that was there. That was quick and painless just like she said it would be. I stood up from the chair and she went over to her work area on the counter. I could tell that she was working with the sample that she had taken. I could only hope that it came back negative. Vain walked over to me and stood next to me but he didn't say a word. I wanted to start a conversation with him, but he didn't seem like he was in the mood. I looked down at my feet and waited patiently for the doctor to give me my results.

"Are the tests usually right," Vain asked the doctor.

"Yes, a blood test is usually not needed. But if you two don't want children then you need to use some sort of protection." She looked at Vain and raised an eyebrow.

He rubbed the back of his neck and smiled, "thanks doc."

She shook her head and smiled at me, "the blood test came back negative. If you're interested in birth control, I can recommend some for you."

I smiled at her weakly, "no thank you. I'm not usually sexually active. This was just an accident."

"I understand," she smiled gathering her things. "Well, if you need me, here is my card. I am always here to help and talk to young women like you." She handed me her card and I took it quickly. She left the house leaving me alone with Vain.

He turned and walked into the living room, and I followed him. Now that I knew that I wasn't pregnant, I could rest easy. I was ready to go home and let things go back to normal.

"Thank you for meeting with me," I smiled grabbing my phone.

He sat down on the couch and stared at me. I stood there feeling uncomfortable waiting for him to say something to me.

"Athena, I want you to leave me alone. I don't want to talk to you unless it's about work. Don't call me or text me unless it's about work. I don't want anything to do with you anymore. Do you understand?"

I nodded my head slowly, "yes I do." I don't know where this was coming from, but I wasn't about to bother him. He was making it clear that he wanted me to stop contacting him. I wasn't the type to hassle anyone, and I wouldn't. I planned on giving him what he wanted.

He pulled his phone out of his pocket, "my driver will take you home."

I rolled my eyes, "I think I can manage on my own. Thanks though for the kind gesture."

I turned to leave but he called my name. I didn't understand him, why was he doing all this? Why would he tell me to leave him alone and then have his driver take me home? He was being rude just to turn around and be nice. It was confusing the hell out of me, and I couldn't stand it anymore.

"LEAVE ME ALONE! JUST STOP, OKAY?" I couldn't help but scream at him. I was heartbroken by his actions, and he didn't care.

He stood up and walked towards me, "stop it."

I shoved him away from, "no you stop it! I'm not a toy that you can use and throw away when it's convenient for you. You tell me to stay away from you but that's all that I've wanted! I wanted you to leave me alone, I wanted you to set me free, but you didn't. YOU'RE SUCH A SELFISH BASTARD AND I HATE THAT I FELL IN LOVE WITH YOU."

He grabbed me by the hair and slammed me against the wall. "You don't think that the feeling is mutual? I fucking fell in love with you too, but I can't be the man you want. I don't do relationships. All that I know how to do is fuck women and use them for what they are good for."

"STAY THE FUCK AWAY FOR ME!" I yelled slapping him across the face. "I hate you…and I want you to stay away from me."

He shoved me away from him, "you don't have to worry about that. I don't intend on fucking you anymore, now get out."

I ran out of his house sobbing loudly. My brother was right, Vain wasn't a good person and he never would be.

Dating

It has been three days since I last talked to Vain. I was heartbroken by the things he said. I was also confused because I didn't understand where all this was coming from. He wanted me to leave him alone, but he wouldn't set me free from the contract. How was I supposed to face him tomorrow? I rolled my eyes and fixed my shirt. I don't know why I was thinking about him when I had a date with Neji. I looked at my reflection in the mirror and smiled. I wore a black crop top with white skinny jeans. The outfit hugged all my small curves and made me feel sexy. My thigh-high black boots completed the look. I ran my fingers through my curly ponytail and smiled. I was perfect. I grabbed my purse and walked down the stairs quickly. I knew that Neji would be popping up any minute and I wanted to be ready. I smiled at Roman and shook my head. He was having a lazy day today and it was nice to see him relaxing. He was working hard these days and he needed a day off.

"Where are you going looking all pretty?"

I smiled and walked up to him placing a kiss on his cheek. "I have a date tonight."

He raised an eyebrow, "with who?"

"Neji Vega. You remember him, right?"

He shrugged, "yea. He seems pretty cool so I can't be upset. Be home by ten."

I frowned, "eleven. I'm almost eighteen and I should be able to stay out late."

"But you're not so come home at ten. Don't argue with me either," he sighed walking away from me.

I rolled my eyes and giggled, "fine. By the way, you look cute in your SpongeBob pajama pants." I could hear him laugh and that made me laugh harder. I was glad that he and I were able to make up and get back on good terms.

The doorbell rang and I rushed to the door to open it. Neji smiled at me and offered me some flowers. I thanked him and took them setting them on the table by the door. Neji looked very handsome tonight. He was a little taller than me and he had long black hair. His green eyes always seemed to glisten with happiness. Overall, he was good looking for a high school boy. Neji and I have been friends since elementary school, and I knew that he always had a crush on me. Joining my dance crew was another way for him to get close to me. He didn't think that I noticed but I did. I stepped outside and closed the door locking it with my key.

"Do you want to see a movie tonight or

dinner?"

I smiled at him, "dinner. I'm so hungry."

He laughed and grabbed my hand leading me over to his car. He opened my door for me, and I climbed in. He closed the door to the car and walked around to his side. He climbed in and I watched him shaking my head. He was nervous and I could tell.

"You don't have to be nervous."

He frowned, "who's nervous, huh?"

I laughed, "you are. I can tell because your cheeks are red."

He started the car and smirked, "they are always red."

The waitress placed our food and drinks in front of us. My stomach was growling so loud that I knew the whole restaurant heard it. Neji kept me distracted by telling me jokes and talking about the past. I grabbed my fork and instantly started to dig into my pasta. I could hear Neji laughing, and I looked at him rolling my eyes.

"Damn, you were hungry."

"Shut up," I giggled.

He took a bite out of his pasta and cleared his throat. "So, have you talked to Roman about college?"

"No, I need to though. I haven't found the right words to say to him."

He grabbed my hand and squeezed it, "he can't keep you caged forever. You have to find your joy in life."

I squeezed his hand back, "you're right. I will talk to him tomorrow and let you know what he says."

"Sounds like a plan."

I looked up and my heart seemed like it stopped

beating. Vain walked into the restaurant with a few of his guy friends. My mind was going crazy. What the hell was he doing here? Why did he have to come to this restaurant out of all restaurants? His eyes locked with mine and he frowned. I knew that seeing me here with Neji was going to piss him off. But who cares? He had no right to be angry especially after he told me to leave him alone. The waitress led them to the table right next to us and I couldn't help but feel the need to throw up. I was trying everything I could to keep my eyes straight ahead. I could smell his cologne and that's when I knew that he was sitting next to me. I could feel his eyes on me, and it made me uncomfortable but I had to stay focused. I had to act as normal as possible.

"Athena."

"Huh," I asked looking at Neji.

He eyed me suspiciously, "are you okay?"

"Oh, yes…I um…I was thinking about what I

was going to do this summer. You're leaving on a family vacation."

He smiled, "yea. I have to go to Fiji with my parents but I'll be back in July."

I sighed, "what am I going to do? Jose is going to California, Sam is going with you, and Eli is going to China. All of you won't be back till July."

"Jealous, huh?" He laughed taking a sip of his drink.

I nodded my head quickly, "of course I am. It's not every day that you get to go to Fiji. You might meet a sexy mermaid and swim away with her."

"Now I know that you're jealous for sure."

I laughed taking another bite out of my pasta. Neji would always be a good friend to me, and I appreciated that. He was comforting me, and he didn't even realize that he was.

"I know that you'll find something to do. You

always do and before you know it, we will be back. You can write me letters and bake me some cookies too."

I rolled my eyes, "I don't bake. But I could try I guess."

"Practice makes perfect, that's what you always tell me."

I smiled, "I see that you pay attention in dance class."

He scoffed, "of course I do. What do you think I did the whole time?"

"You would be back there talking to Sam about the pretty new cheerleaders. I quote, they are sexy as hell man, end quote."

He laughed, "no. no.no. You have it all wrong. Sam was talking to me about the cheerleaders. I was just listening," he held his hands up in surrender.

"Yeah right, so what were you talking about then?"

He smirked, "you really want to know?"

"Mhm," I nodded my head.

He leaned in close and looked both ways, "I was talking about food." He whispered.

I covered my mouth and laughed, "what the hell? Why did you have to whisper food?"

He shrugged, "everyone can't know my secret."

I took another bite out of my food and watched as he ate his. It was nice catching up with him and being normal. I felt like a normal teenager when I was with my dance crew. I didn't feel like I was mixed in mafia bullshit.

"Honestly, I talked to Sam about you. I wanted to know if I had a chance with you or not."

I looked down at my hands, "why didn't you ask?"

"I didn't want to ruin the friendship that we had. I wasn't always faithful, you know. I didn't want to break your heart, but I know now that would never happen. If given the chance to be with you, I would cherish you."

I rested my face against the palm of my hand. I wasn't used to getting treated like this and it was new to me. Neji was very sweet, but I knew that I couldn't just jump into a relationship with him. Maybe, we could work our way up to that point.

"We will see," I mumbled. "I wonder if you love food more than me?"

He smirked, "are you kidding? Come on, who doesn't love food more than anything?"

"You have proved a major point."

We both laughed and continued our dinner. I could still feel Vain's eyes on me from time to time, but I did everything I could to ignore him. He wasn't important and I would not let him ruin my night. After we finished eating, we stood up from the table and left the restaurant. It was nine-thirty and I needed to get home by ten. My phone started to ring and when I looked

down it was Vain. I declined the call quickly
and turned my phone off. Neji asked me if
everything was okay, and I nodded my head.
My night was coming to an end, and I wouldn't
ruin it by thinking about Vain.

I walked into my bedroom and threw my purse
on the bed. Tonight, was fun and I really
enjoyed myself. Neji gave me a good night kiss
and I touched my lips thinking about it. I
removed my boots and went into the bathroom
to turn on my shower water. When I came into
the house it was dark and quiet. I didn't see
Roman's car here in the driveway. I turned my
phone back on to see a text message from him.
He said that he decided to go out with a few
friends and wouldn't stay out too late. I replied
to his text and told him that I made it home
safely and everything was locked up. I removed

my clothes and grabbed my towel wrapping it around my body. I was about to go into the bathroom, but I heard footsteps in the hallway. I frowned and opened my bedroom door to peek out but to my surprise, no one was there.

I walked to the top of the stairs looking around. "ROMAN, IS THAT YOU?" I waited patiently for a response but nothing. I shrugged and walked back into my bedroom closing and locking the door. I always locked my bedroom door when I was home alone. We had a great security system, but I didn't always trust technology.

I turned around and froze when I saw Vain sitting on my bed. I wanted to run but I felt like I was paralyzed. I backed away slowly as he came closer to me. Why was he here? Was it because I was denying his calls?

"Vain, what are you doing here?"

He didn't say anything which scared me further. He cupped my chin forcing me to look at him. "Do you think it's okay to embarrass me?"

"I don't know what you're talking about." I tried to step past him, but he blocked my way.

"Did you enjoy acting like a slut tonight?"

"Excuse me? Listen, you don't come into my home and disrespect me. I am single and I can do whatever I want to do. You told me to leave you alone and that's what I was doing."

He grabbed a fistful of my hair and yanked hard. "SHUT THE FUCK UP. I do what I want when I want. You think you can just go around acting like a little whore and embarrassing me? You think that shit is funny, huh? You told me three days ago that you were pregnant. How the hell do I know that the pregnancy scare you had was from me? You're fucking him, right? It could have been his child and you're crying to me."

"Why the hell would I lie about being pregnant by you? What do you take me for? I'm not one of those whores that try to trap men with children. I don't care about having a child by you. If I was having sex with Neji and I thought that I was pregnant, I would have told him. I don't have to lie and cover-up bullshit. The only man that I've been with is you. You can believe what you want, I don't care." I shoved him away from me and he smirked. I wanted to slap him across the face. How dare he come into my home and treat me like this.

"Stop lying to me, Amore. I know that you opened your legs to him. You opened your legs so easily to me." He licked his lips and grabbed my towel yanking it away from my body.

I balled my hands into fists and covered myself. "Get out. Get out of my house now. I will call my brother and tell him that."

"Tell him how I fucked you. Tell him how I almost got you pregnant," he chuckled. He grabbed me and pulled me against his body. "Tell him how many times I've been inside you while you're at it." He stroked my cheek with the back of his hand softly. "You will learn not to threaten me."

I looked away for him without saying another word. It was useless and it didn't matter anymore. I was tired of fighting with him. I wanted these six months to be over, but I knew even then that he wouldn't leave me alone.

"Speechless?" he smiled kissing my forehead.

"What do you want?"

He cocked his head over to the side, "you. I want you on that bed right now."

"No, I'm not allowing you to have sex with me anymore. I told you that I would work for you. You told me to keep it about business and that is what I'm doing. You having sex with me is personal."

He sighed, "are you denying me?"

I stared at him confused. He either was in denial, or he was stupid. Of course, I was denying him. "Yea I am. Sex is not in our contract, and you know it."

He chuckled and licked his lips, "hmm it seems you're right. No worries though, Amore. You'll be in my bed soon enough and if you don't…well, I'll make sure that you're in someone else's."

He left my bedroom before I could question him. What the hell did he mean by someone else's? What would he do? How far was he willing to go? Why would he tell me to leave him alone just to threaten me? I rubbed my head and sat on the bed slowly. What was my life turning into?

Back to work

As much as I wanted to enjoy the rest of my weekend, I couldn't. I was back at the club for my shift, and I dreaded it. Vain popped up after my date with Neji and things didn't go well. I didn't know what he had planned, and I didn't want to know. I planned to stay out of the way as much as I could. If I avoided him then he wouldn't be able to bother me. I already had it planned that when I saw him, I would go in the opposite direction. I ran my fingers through my hair and stepped into the club. It was empty and I was shocked. I had to be here early so that I could set up for tonight. I dropped my bag on the counter and started to pull the chairs off the tables. The club was clean for the most part, so the only thing that I would have to do is wipe down the tables and stuff. I sighed and walked around each table pulling the chairs down. I was ready for this night to be over and then I would spend the rest of my night cuddled up in bed. I planned on watching a few more Inuyasha episodes when I got home. I was almost done with the series, and I was excited to see what happened next. The last episode I watched was when Sesshomaru tried to save Kagura from dying. The door opened and I turned around to see Roxy come in. She looked at me and rolled her eyes and I ignored her. I continued to pull the chairs down quickly. The sooner I got done, the sooner I could go and sit in my little corner and hide.

"Vain was talking about firing someone yesterday. I hope it's you."

I rolled my eyes and turned to face her, "me too."

She frowned, "you're weird."

I placed my hand on my hip, "how? Just because I don't talk to you doesn't mean I'm weird."

She raised an eyebrow, "you're weird because you keep chasing a man that doesn't want you."

I shook my head and turned to walk away from her. I was not about to have this conversation with her again. It was pointless and I didn't understand why she kept trying to rub it in my face that she had Vain. I would be happy if he gave her all his attention instead of stalking me. I wish that he would leave me alone and stop breaking into my house and threatening me. She obviously didn't know the whole truth and I was not about to explain it to her.

The front door opened, and I turned to see Vain. He was on the phone and Roxy instantly ran to his side. I pretended not to notice them and continued to pull the chairs down.

"Dimmelo dopo," Vain sighed ending the call.

Roxy grabbed his arm, "I'm so glad that you're here. Baby doll threatened to slap me. I didn't do anything to her at all. The only thing that I said was do you need some help and she told me to leave her alone before she slapped me."

I turned around quickly, and my mouth fell open. She couldn't be serious, right? Was she really going to play this innocent act in front of Vain and paint me out to be the bad guy? Vain looked at me and I could see the anger in his eyes. He stepped towards me, and I stood my ground because I knew that I had nothing to hide. She was lying and it was clear.

"Why the hell would you threaten her?"

"I didn't," I said turning my back to him. I continued to pull the chairs down quickly. I knew that he was upset that I brushed him off without fully explaining what happened. I didn't see the point when he was going to side with her anyway.

He grabbed my arm roughly yanking me

towards him. "Ow, you're hurting me," I hissed trying to get my arm free.

He closed his eyes taking a deep breath, "I'm going to ask you one more time. Why did you threaten her?"

I looked into his eyes, "I didn't. I came in and started to work. She came in and started to taunt me, she called me weird and the only thing I did was walk away. I would never threaten anyone. You can check the cameras because that never happened."

He let me go and walked towards the stairs, "I'll look at the cameras. Finish working and get ready for tonight, both of you."

I rubbed my arm watching him climb the stairs quickly. I knew that Roxy felt like an idiot knowing that she would be caught in a lie. I had nothing to lie about, and I knew that he would see that too. Hopefully, he would feel like a piece of crap after watching the cameras. I looked at Roxy and she looked pissed off, but I didn't care. She deserved whatever punishment that Vain was going to give her.

I looked at my reflection in the mirror gulped. This outfit was nothing like the outfits that I've worn before. It was a black lace bodysuit. That showed a lot of skin. I wore some black and silver heels to match. My hair was down, and it was curled to perfection. My makeup was done to perfection as well. My eyes were black with glitter. With red lipstick to match.

"Damn, you look good baby doll." Diamond smiled helping me touch up my outfit.

I stared at my reflection in the mirror, "I don't know. I feel like I'm showing too much."

She laughed, "If you want to make money you have to show more than that." She was very sexy tonight. She had on a pink thong with

some glitter nipple stickers to cover her nipples.
She wore silver nine-inch heels to complete her
outfit. Her hair was silky straight, and her
glitter makeup added to her look for tonight.

I looked her up and down, "you always look
good."

She giggled, "thank you, baby." She grabbed
my hand, "good luck tonight. Be careful,
okay?"

I nodded my head quickly and watched her
leave. I was the only one left in the dressing
room. I knew that I couldn't stand in here
forever. Vain would come looking for me and I
didn't want him to do that. I took a deep breath
and walked towards the door. It was now or
never and so I swallowed my pride and stepped
outside the dressing room.

I walked over to the bar and grabbed the tray
that was waiting on me. I knew that I had to
pass out drinks and I needed to get started. I
took the tray and walked around to each table

offering drinks. Men were happy to take the drinks from me even though their eyes never left the stage. I smiled at them trying my best to be polite. I didn't want to be complained on because that would attract Vain. I walked over to a table and rolled my eyes when I saw Vain sitting there. He was talking to Adonis and that made my heart pound even harder. The last time that I saw him, things did not end well for me or him. He got a drink thrown on him and he deserved it, but I knew better this time. There was another man sitting at the table with them, but I wasn't sure who he was. There was a woman who was sitting next to Vain, and he had his arm around her. He was whispering something in her ear, and she was blushing. I knew that he was doing this on purpose, and I didn't care. I was going to beat him at his own game and show him how unbothered I was. I walked up to the table and offered them drinks and that instantly got Vain's attention. He told the girl to leave, and she stood up instantly. She walked away from the table, and I gulped setting the drinks down in front of them. I was trying to be careful because I was shaking. I didn't want to accidentally spill a drink on them. I was about to walk away but Vain grabbed my hand.

"Adonis, I think that you should have a little fun with baby doll."

I stared at him confused because I didn't know what he meant. What did he mean have fun?

Adonis chuckled, "I would be honored."

"Then she is yours for the night," Vain smiled.

What the hell was he talking about? There is no way that he was going to lay a finger on me. I finally found my voice after a minute, "no. If you touch me, I'll cut your fucking fingers off."

Adonis laughed, "ohh she is feisty."

Vain rubbed his chin, "hmm, I would love to cut of Neji's fingers. He is currently with one of my men so all it takes is one phone call."

"What the hell are you talking about?" What the hell did he mean that he had Neji?

"You heard me, I have your little boyfriend and I won't hesitate to kill him. You do what I say, and he lives."

My heart seemed like it stopped in my chest. Why was he doing this? Was all of this because I wouldn't sleep with him? I didn't understand what more he wanted. I was here working for him and that should be enough. "What do you want?"

He picked up his drink slowly, "sit on Adonis's lap. Let him touch you wherever he wants. You will act like the little whore you are. You acted like one yesterday so this should be easy."

I placed the tray of drinks on the empty table next to me. I wanted to cry but I knew that I had to be strong. There was no way that I was going to allow him to see that he got to me. I sat down in Adonis's lap slowly and he groaned grabbing me by the throat. He pushed my head over to the side and placed soft kisses on my neck. My body was trembling, and I knew that he could tell.

"You're so fucking sexy," he breathed against my ear. "I'm glad that Vain finally decided to share you." He spread my legs roughly and I closed my eyes tight.

"Please stop," I whispered. I didn't want him to touch me. I couldn't stop the vomit that was going to come up. I was trying so hard not to be scared but I was. I knew that Vain would always protect me and I felt safe with him. But now he was staring at me and watching as I got violated.

"She's scared," Adonis chuckled nibbling on my earlobe.

I looked into Vain's eyes, and I could see that he didn't care. He shrugged and gulped down his drink. I knew that I didn't have a choice but to endure it because I knew that Neji's life was in danger. I didn't want him to get hurt because of me. He didn't deserve it and it was my fault that he was in this mess.

"Go get me another drink," Adonis whispered turning my face towards his. I tried to stand up, but he stopped me. I hardly had a moment to react before he smashed his lips against mine. I felt him press his tongue to the seam of my lips and at my grant of access, he delved inside my mouth. I didn't want to upset him, and I knew that denying him would be bad. If I wasn't making him happy then Vain would hurt Neji. He rested his hand below my ear, his thumb caressing my cheek gently. I could nearly feel the slight burn of the alcohol, as it rolled off his tongue and seeped down my throat with every push of his tongue against mine. He bit my bottom lip and sucked it between his lips. When he pulled away our eyes met, and he frowned. My cheeks were on fire, and I knew it was because I was flustered. The kiss was a passionate kiss and that shocked me. I could tell that it shocked him too.

"Go," he whispered.

I didn't wait to be told twice. I stood up quickly and walked away from the table. I could feel his eyes on me and Vain's eyes, but I didn't look back. I touched my lips slowly and shook my head. What was that?

Attacked

The club was empty, and everyone had left. I knew that Vain and a few of the guys were upstairs talking about business. I was left cleaning the club after everyone was gone. I placed all the chairs on the tables and mopped the floor. I cleaned the bar, bathrooms, and the stage. Now I was headed to the backroom to clean them. I didn't like cleaning the backrooms because there would always be men's sperm on the floor. It was disgusting and I hated it, but I knew I had to get it cleaned. There were five private rooms and the quicker

that I finished the sooner I could go home. It
was three in the morning, and I knew that
Roman would be texting me if he got home and
I wasn't there. I walked into the first backroom
and to my surprise it was clean. It hadn't been
used which was good for me. I walked out and
pushed the door open to the second one. I
smiled when I noticed that this one was also
clean. I knew that the girls were helping me out
secretly and I appreciated that. I left and pushed
the door open to the third one. This one was a
little messy but nothing major. I started to fix
the pillows on the couch quickly. I hated being
back here by myself because it creeped me out.
I grabbed the mop and started to mop the floor
quickly. The men didn't have any type of
consideration at all. They would just release on
the floor and then they would leave. It was not
sanitary, and it showed they were not clean at
all. I tucked a strand of hair behind my ear and
dropped the mop back in the soppy water. This
room was clean for the most part so it was time
to move on to room four. I walked out of the

room and pushed open the door to the fourth private area. This one was clean and there was a note on the door. I picked it up and looked down at it. It was from kitten, and she drew a smiley face. I knew that she had cleaned the room for me. I would have to thank her when I saw her again. I walked into the fifth room and rolled my eyes. This one was very messy, but it wasn't too bad. It would take me about ten minutes to get it cleaned.

I started to fix the pillows on the couch quickly. I jumped when I heard the door close. I turned around and frowned when I saw a man leaning against the door. He was tall and very handsome. He was covered in tattoos, and I knew that he had to be a part of the mafia. He had short black hair and dark green eyes. I tried to study his face to see if I knew him from somewhere, but I didn't.

"I'm sorry but the club is closed,"

He smiled and took a step towards me, "is it?"

I walked around the couch slowly. I was trying to create some distance between us. I had to try to stay away from him. I cursed under my breath when I realized that I didn't have my phone on me. I was in this room with a strange man and no way out.

"I have to go but if you need anything the owner is upstairs." I tried to walk towards the door as fast as I could, but he grabbed me by the arm.

"Why are you trying to leave so soon? I just got here, and I would like for you to stay and keep me company." He caressed my cheek with the back of his hand.

I shook my head, "I'm sorry but I can't. The club is closed, so please let me go."

He sighed, "I don't think so. I came here for something, and I plan on getting it."

Everything happened so fast after he said those words. He shoved me on the couch and climbed on top of me pinning me down. I could feel him grabbing at my bodysuit and hearing it rip. I couldn't think straight anymore. The only thing on my mind was surviving and getting away from this man. A loud shrilling scream escaped from deep within my throat as he placed himself between my legs and clawed at my skin. I felt him spread my legs as he forced kisses all over my neck. I kept pushing against his chest as best as I could. He was like a brick wall, and he wasn't moving.

"LET GO OF ME NOW!" I screamed trying to move my body away from him.

"Shut the hell up," he growled slapping me across the face.

The slap caught me off guard and due to the impact, I felt the room spinning and it seemed like I lost my voice. I held my face trying to get myself to focus. My consciousness was fading in and out due to the adrenaline running through my veins. Tears clogged my vision and my fighting faded slowly. The only sound left was my whimpers as I felt him kiss down to my body.

"Please, I whispered. "Please you don't have to do this. Please don't do this...please," I sobbed pushing against his body.

I heard him unbuckle his belt and I knew what was going to happen next. He forced my legs open even further and I screamed again. He quickly covered my mouth to silence me.

"Please," I screamed against his hand.

"How do you want it?" He laughed pushing my bodysuit to the side. I sobbed softly closing my eyes tight. "I can be as rough as you want, or I can make love to you." He breathed against my ear.

I shook my head trying to answer his question. I wanted to leave but I knew that he wasn't going to let that happen.

"NO," I screamed when I felt his fingers invade my body.

"You're tight," he groaned. "I hope that you

can handle me."

I felt like I was going to throw up. No man had touched me like this before. The only man that I ever allowed to do this was Vain. I felt violated and dirty, and I knew that I would hate myself if he penetrated me. He rubbed himself against me and that's when I started to fight him once again. I couldn't let this happen to me. I wasn't about to be raped in a strip club. I closed my eyes and brought my knee up quickly. I heard him groan and all his body weight was suddenly gone. I opened my eyes to see him on the floor in pain and I took that as my chance to get up and run to get help. I closed the door and locked it with the keys, and I could hear him banging on it from the other side. My body was shaking all over and I could barely see or walk.

"OPEN THIS FUCKING DOOR. YOU STUPID LITTLE BITCH! I'M GOING TO FIND YOU AND KILL YOU. YOU BETTER HOPE THAT I FUCK YOU FIRST."

I ran to the stairs and climbed them quickly. I

was shaking so bad that I didn't think that I would make it to the top. I was sobbing uncontrollably, and I wanted to get to a safe place. I saw Vain's office, and I didn't bother knocking on the door. I turned the knob and walked in without a second thought. There were five men in the room, Vain, Adonis, Ace, and the other two I didn't recognize. They turned to look at me, but my eyes never left Vain's.

"I...was just...I...I. He touched me and I tried...I couldn't." I placed my hand on my stomach sobbing loudly. I couldn't even find the words to say.

Adonis stood up, "what happened?"

"He tried to...r-rape me."

Ace and the two men that I didn't know stood up and raced out of the room. Adonis walked over to me wrapping his jacket around me. He left telling Vain that he was going to find out who the man was. Vain walked towards me and I stepped back quickly. I was scared and I didn't want to be touched right now.

"Stay here," he said before walking out the room and closing the door.

VAIN POV

Ace was able to get the man who touched Athena. I was pissed off and I felt disrespected. How dare he come in here and place his hands on my girl. How dare he try to force himself inside her. He was going to pay for this, and I hoped he knew that. I walked to the basement of the club and balled my hands into fists. My blood was boiling, and I couldn't think straight. Seeing Athena run into my office like that broke my heart. Her clothes were ripped, and scratches covered her body. I knew that he had hit her due to her face being swollen. I ran my fingers through my hair and cursed loudly. Adonis had his sleeves rolled up and his knuckles were bloody from hitting the guy over and over again. I looked at the guy and I didn't recognize him. Who the hell was he and who did he work for? Why was he at my club after hours and what would make him think it was okay to attack someone on my property? He was asking to die, and he was going to get his wish tonight.

"Who are you?"

He laughed; you can call me Blue."

"Why the fuck are you here? Why did you attack my girl? Answer those questions before I shoot you in the fucking head."

"Your girl huh? Well, she was delicious. I really enjoyed fucking her."

I balled my hand up and punched him in the jaw. This guy had a lot of nerve talking reckless to me.

Ace smirked and lit a cigarette, "I think he works for Romano now. He used to work with you and his name was Drew. I guess Romano offered him more money."

I ran my hand over my face and took a deep breath. There was no end to the shit this guy would do. He has been a real pain in my ass these past few months. He stole from me and now he was trying to rape my girl. This guy was a former worker of mine. He was always sneaky, but I never knew he would cross this line. There was more to this story, but I knew that he wouldn't tell me.

"How did you find out about her? Have you been watching me?"

He licked the blood off his lip, "everyone in the mafia knows about your love affair with Athena Vintalli."

Adonis looked at me in shock, "what the fuck? Athena Vintalli? You can't be fucking serious? Tell me this guy is joking? That is Roman's little sister, what are you doing? SHE IS SEVENTEEN! I just fucking kissed her and touched her, Vain. I have no issue with the Vintalli family, and I don't want one either."

I placed my hand on my head, "look I'll explain later."

"Hell no, we are going to talk right now. You put her in danger, and you don't see that. She is at risk, Vain! The Vintalli family is the most honorable family in the mafia. They have no enemies for a reason."

I growled and slammed my hand down on the desk. "I know that I fucked up big time. I should have stayed away from her which is why I'm trying to."

"If you were trying to stay away from her then you would. She shouldn't have been here tonight, and you know it." He folded his arms across his chest.

"I love her," I looked at him. I couldn't hide it anymore. But I knew that me loving her was dangerous.

He placed his hand on my shoulder, "we will talk later. Finish off this bastard."

I walked over to the guy and took the gun that
Ace handed me. I pointed the gun at Drew's
head and pulled the trigger. A loud bang echoed
through the room and his body went limp
against the restraints.

"Get rid of him," I mumbled walking towards
the stairs. I needed to check on Athena. I
walked up the stairs quickly and back to my
office. I wanted to make sure that she was okay.
I hated myself for what happened to her, and I
couldn't blame anyone but myself. I pushed
open my office door and looked around the
room. I could feel my heart racing as I searched
the room for her. I spotted her asleep on the
couch and I smiled weakly.

I walked over to her and placed my hand on her
cheek. "I'm sorry that I put in danger. I can't
explain what's going on but trust me, I'll keep
you safe. I love you…I really do. I can't be
with you, and I hate it but it's for your safety." I
placed a kiss on her forehead before picking her
up bridal style. I needed to get her home before

her brother started to worry about her. Besides,
I had business that I had to take care of. No one
was going to hurt her, and I was going to make
sure of that.

Afraid

It has been three weeks since I was attacked at the club. Vain hasn't been to the club for the past three weekends. I haven't been able to sleep properly since that night. I can still feel his hands on me sometimes and it's scary. I can't forget the words that he spoke to me while he violated me. Since the attack, I haven't been staying late at the club. Vain hired other women to clean the club. I still have to show up for work and that drives me crazy. I hate being in there and it causes me to remember that night. The only person that I told was Kitten. I knew that I could trust her, and she wouldn't tell anyone else. Vain didn't want me telling anyone because he said that he didn't want to scare the other workers. He said that he didn't want any negative energy directed towards his club. He didn't tell me this in person, he sent me a text message. I've been wanting to talk to him, but he hasn't been at the club. I didn't feel safe anymore and the only thing I wanted to do was hide in my house. Roman was a little suspicious but he didn't push the issue. I sighed and ran my fingers through my hair. I needed to get out of the house and stop living in fear. I couldn't be like this forever because it would only hurt me in the end. I decided that I would spend a day with him. He wanted to spend some time with me before he left for Fiji with Sam and his family. I took one last look at myself in the mirror and smiled. I wasn't going to focus on Vain or what happened that night. I wanted to spend some well needed time with Neji and focus on him. I was over Vain and all his asshole ways. I couldn't forgive him, not after what he did. Yes, he saved me but that would have never happened if it wasn't for him. If I wasn't cleaning the club late at night for him, I would have been at home safe. I didn't want to be with Vain anymore. The only thing I wanted was to finish the six months and move on. Neji was sweet and he treated me the way that I was supposed to be treated. I didn't feel like I was one out of a million girls. It was a good thing that Vain, and I weren't talking because it made it easier for me to move on.

I grabbed Neji's hand and laughed as we walked down the street. He shook his head and continued to laugh at his own joke about Sam. We finished lunch and now we were headed to his house to watch a movie. I didn't want to be in a movie theater. I wanted to have some alone time with Neji.

"I'm glad that you asked me to come out with you."

I frowned, "you asked me out."

He chuckled kissing my hand, "I'm glad that you agreed to come."

I looked at him and smiled, "you missed me, huh?"

He scoffed, "of course I did. The last time that we went out was three weeks ago. I'll be leaving for Fiji soon and I wanted to see you."

I laid my head on his shoulder, "I hate that you're leaving."

"I'll be back before you know it, Athena." He kissed the top of my head.

"I'll make sure to call you twenty times a day," I giggled.

He placed his hand on his chin, "call forty. Twenty is not enough."

I shook my head and laughed, "ok."

Being like this with Neji was so normal. It felt nice and I loved the feeling. I didn't have to worry about him yelling at me. I didn't have to worry about the mafia either. It was just me and him and I was grateful for that. I was depressed that he was leaving because I would be alone for the whole summer. The only thing I would be able to do would be to sit around the house. I sighed and looked down at my feet, I hated being in the mafia. Why couldn't my life be normal? All my friends had normal lives and they got to do normal stuff. It was unfair and I hated it sometimes.

"You know, I can ask my parents can you come."

I looked up at Neji, "thank you but I couldn't. As much as I want to I can't. Roman would not let that happen and besides, I have to be here to help him. When he is not home, someone has to watch the house."

He shrugged, "I understand that. Your house is big as hell. Your dad must have been a top doctor."

I laughed, "yea something like that."

No one knew that my family was involved in the mafia. The only person who knew was Tarma. I knew that I could be putting their life in danger if they knew. Neji's parents were big lawyers and they worked with cops. It wasn't a safe situation for him or them. I guess that's why I never pursued him. I knew that I couldn't be with a normal guy. The mafia is where I belonged and there was no escaping that. Neji put his arm around me and smiled. I leaned closer to him and closed my eyes.

I walked towards the club and sighed. I was on my way back to work, and I hated it. I bit my lip and closed my eyes remembering last night with Neji. We went back to his house to watch

Jumanji. The whole movie he was touching me and kissing on me. I was getting turned on quickly and I tried to fight it. One thing led to another, and we started to kiss. I climbed on top of him, and his hands roamed all over my body. I wanted him, there was no doubt in my mind. Our kissing led to our clothes being taken off. He flipped us over and started to kiss down my body. I moaned loudly and I regretted it because his family was downstairs. I closed my eyes and bit my lip when I felt his lips on my inner thigh. He was teasing me, and I hated it so much. When I felt him grip my thigh roughly, I freaked out. I moved away from him quickly trying to cover myself. He asked me if I was okay and I told him yes, but I lied. I wanted to go through with it but the night I got attacked flashed in my brain. I apologized to him and grabbed my clothes running into the bathroom. I shook my head and rolled my eyes. I felt so damn embarrassed and pathetic. I couldn't do anything because I was afraid. I shouldn't have been afraid because it was Neji, but I was. I didn't know how to face him or what to say to him after that. He told me that it was fine when he dropped me off at home, but I didn't feel that way. I knew that he was upset with me, and he had every right to be.

I pulled open the doors to the club and stepped in quickly. I looked up and to my surprise, Vain was at the bar. I hadn't seen him in three weeks, so it was weird seeing him. I was scared of what he would say when he noticed me standing there. He was on the phone, and it seemed like it was an important call. He looked up and our eyes met. I would be lying if I said I didn't feel some kind of way. I missed him in a weird way, but I knew that I couldn't be with him. He didn't want me anyway so why did it matter?

"Athena, you're just in time to help me."

I turned around and smiled at Kitten. She was standing there with her hand on her hip smiling. Kitten and I have been close since I started working here. I was grateful to have someone that I could talk to. I never felt lonely when she was here, and I got through my shift with no problem.

"Did you have fun with Neji?" She smirked wiggling her eyebrows.

"Yes, it was nice. We watched that new Jumanji movie and it was really funny."

She frowned, "so you two didn't have sex?"

I grabbed her arm and pulled her towards the dressing room. The last thing I wanted to talk about was sex with another man. Vain was standing too close and I didn't want to hear his mouth about me and Neji. She laughed and started to tease me about how I finally lost my V card.

I pulled her over to her makeup vanity and sighed. "I couldn't do it."

She frowned, "what do you mean you couldn't? Were you nervous or was he too little down there?" She raised an eyebrow and crossed her arms over her chest.

I laughed and smacked her arm playfully, "no. He was definitely a great size down there. I had another panic attack and so I stopped him. I ran and hid away in the bathroom for fifteen minutes."

"Really?"

I nodded my head, "I can't do anything Kitten. I can't even bring myself to an orgasm. Every time I touch myself, I feel him. I can hear his voice and it scares me. He told me that he was going to kill me, and I can't live knowing that he is out there."

She pulled me into a hug and rubbed my back. "You have to talk to Vain. I know that you don't want to, but you have to. You can't live your life like this. Especially if you can't have sex."

I rolled my eyes, and I could hear her laughing. I loved Kitten and I knew that she was coming from a good place. She was the only person that

I trusted with my secrets. We hung out a lot now that we were friends. I knew that I could always count on her to make me feel better. She placed a kiss on my cheek and slapped me on the butt.

"Go talk to him now."

I laughed and took a deep breath, "okay."

I knocked on his office door and I heard him say come in. I was nervous because I didn't know what he was going to say. I didn't want to talk to him, but I knew that I didn't have an option. He was sitting at his desk looking down at his phone. There was an empty shot glass in front of him and I knew that he was drinking. He didn't pay me any attention at all and that made me want to turn around and leave. I closed my eyes tight and balled up my fists. No, I had to do this.

"Vain, I hate to bother you, but I need to talk to you. I haven't been able to…I'm afraid."

He looked up and placed his hand on his chin, "of what?"

I frowned, "um…I was attacked by a man here."

He shrugged, "okay that was three weeks ago."

I couldn't believe what I was hearing. Was he really brushing it off as if it was nothing? He didn't care at all, and he was proving that.

"He said that he would kill me. I don't know if he is still out there, and I fear for my life. If you don't care about me then at least care about the fact that it is your fault."

He stood up, "how is that my fault."

"I tried to pay you off and leave but you wouldn't let me. You forced me to stay late and clean the club. You purposely gave me less and less clothes to wear. If you would have let me go a long time ago this wouldn't have happened." I wasn't trying to attack him, but he needed to know the truth.

He walked towards me quickly, "that has nothing to do with me."

I stared at him and crossed my arms over my chest. "You are unbelievable." I turned around to leave but was yanked back roughly by my hair.

"You don't walk away from me. I wasn't finished talking to you," he growled nibbling on my ear. "You don't have to worry about him because I shot his ass. I watched the life drain from his eyes for what he did to you. You should be grateful for that, Amore."

"It still doesn't change the fact that."

He picked me up and lifted me on to his desk with ease. "Change the fact of what?" He whispered brushing his lips against mine. "Listen, it's not my fault that your little boyfriend can't fuck you. Don't try to blame it on the attack either. I found my way between your pretty little legs with ease, and you know what?" He placed soft kisses on my jawline before traveling down to my neck. I closed my eyes tight and moaned softly as he started to suck on my skin.

"I'll do it again," he whispered connecting his lips with mine.

A new Devil

I stared at my reflection in the mirror and smiled. Tonight, I was wearing a dark blue bodysuit that was covered in black leopard print. It was long-sleeved and very sexy. The top part made my boobs look bigger and nicer than they were, which is always a bonus. My black heels wrapped around my lower leg and added to the outfit perfectly. I was nervous because everyone was buzzing about how busy we were going to be tonight. They said that Vain wanted nothing but the best from us. Tonight, the club was going to be filled with very important men. These very important men

had millions of dollars as well. I rolled my eyes
just thinking about it. Great, now I had to be
surrounded by men who were perverts and had
nothing better to do than throw money away at
a strip club. Kitten walked over to me and
whistled, and I laughed shaking my head. She
was dressed in a red lace bra with red lace
panties to match. Her silver nine-inch heels
went perfectly with her lingerie. All the girls
were wearing barely anything, and I was
shocked by that.

"You look cute, but you're never going to make
money all covered up baby doll." Kitten smiled
helping me fix my hair.

"Who is going to be here tonight?" I asked
ignoring her comment.

She smirked, "mafia men." She stood behind
me and stared at me in the mirror. "Be good to
them and they will be good to you. Tonight, is a
big night for Vain. He doesn't want us to
embarrass him at all. Just go out there and do
your job and you'll be fine."

I bit my lip, "that's easier said than done."

She giggled and grabbed my arm pulling me towards the door. "Don't be nervous, you don't have to be. Just think of it as another night at the club. It's just mafia men here instead of normal men. Nothing to be scared about, right?"

She patted me on the back and walked out. I watched as she made her way over to a table full of men. Kitten was shy but she lost that shyness when it came to making money. I smiled at her when she turned around and winked at me. I was stalling in the doorway, and I knew that I shouldn't. If Vain saw me standing here and not passing out drinks, he would be pissed off. I took a deep breath and mumbled to myself that it was just another night. I walked over to the bar quickly and smiled at the woman who was getting my tray ready for me. I looked across the room and I spotted Vain. He was sitting with Adonis and Ace. I couldn't help but bit my lip as my mind

went back to earlier. He was one step away
from having sex with me and then Ace knocked
on the door. I was glad because I didn't want to
have sex with him. It was hard telling Vain no
because he hated it. It made him angry, and I
hated making him angry. Whenever he would
get mad at me, it wouldn't end well. What
confused me the most was that he touched me
easily and I let him. Neji touched me and I
freaked out. What was the difference between
the two? Could it be the fact that Vain took my
virginity and I still had that connection to him
even though I didn't want to? I shook my head
and sighed; it didn't matter. I picked the tray up
off the bar counter and started to walk around
offering drinks. Men took the drinks and didn't
turn their attention to me which was great. I
didn't like it when men looked at me or tried to
touch me. I walked towards a table in the back
and tried to seem as nice as possible. The man
sitting at the table was sexy as hell. He had
short black hair that was shaved on the sides
and the back. The rest of his hair at the top was

combed neatly over to the side. He had tattoos that covered his arms and his hands. His white t-shirt couldn't hide the build of his body. I could literally see every inch of muscle and the outline of his abs. He had a small tattoo above his left eyebrow that said this is art. He had a small amount of facial hair but not much. I didn't care for facial hair, but it fit his face perfectly. My heart seemed like it was pounding in my chest the closer I got to him. Who was he? When his light brown eyes looked up at me, I almost tripped and fell. He was beyond sexy if that was even possible. I stood in front of the table, and we stared at each other. I wanted to ask him if he wanted a drink, but I couldn't seem to form the words. No man had ever made me this nervous, except Vain.

"Are you going to offer me a drink?"

I almost dropped the tray when he spoke to me. He had a very thick and heavy Spanish accent. His voice held dominance and I could sense it. He raised an eyebrow when I didn't respond to him. I didn't want to come off disrespectful, so I cleared my throat and took a drink of the tray.

"You didn't have to ask; I knew you wanted one." I smiled at him politely.

He smirked, "Is that so?"

I nodded my head and turned to leave. The sooner I got away from him the better. He was dangerous and there was no doubt about it. I wanted to ask his name, but I didn't want to be rude in any way.

"What is your name, baby girl?"

I turned to face him, "Baby doll. Can I get you another drink?"

He shook his head and leaned back in his seat. "No, but I do want you to take a seat."

I looked around quickly, "I'm sorry I have to get back to work. My boss would kill me if he saw me slacking on the drinks."

"I'm sure your boss won't mind. You're taking

care of one of his customers, no?"

I took a deep breath and sat down quickly. I didn't understand why he wanted me here with him. What could be his motive? I looked at all the other girls dancing and smiled. They were having a good time because of all the money they were getting. I knew that they would be satisfied when they went to the back to count their money.

"Why do you work here?"

I turned my attention towards him, "I needed extra money."

He picked up his drink and gulped it down quickly. "You're too sexy to be working in a place like this. You should come work at my club. You will make way more money."

"I'll be leaving the strip club business in four months. Thanks for the offer though," I smiled playing with my hands.

"Pity," he mumbled.

"What's your name?" I frowned staring at him.

"You don't need to know my name. Knowing my name is dangerous and useless."

I nodded my head slowly, "okay."

He laughed, "are you always this polite?"

"Not always but I try to be," I smiled.

He grabbed a shot glass near him and gulped down the drink inside. I watched him and tried my best to be as nice as possible. I was ready to get up and leave but I didn't want to leave without being told. We sat in silence for a while, and I was grateful for that. I didn't like telling my whole life story to a stranger. A man in a black suit walked over to the table.

"Boss, it's time."

He stood up and I stared up at him. He was tall just like Vain and that made me clench my legs together. He was a stranger, but he was turning me on slowly. He turned to face me, and I bit my lip nervously.

"Baby girl, thank you for your company. Here is a little something to show my gratitude." He pulled something out his jacket pocket and slowly stuck it in the middle of my boobs. He cupped my chin forcing me to look at him. "Stai attento…ti fidi facilmente."

I frowned and watched him walk away. I didn't speak Italian but now I wanted to. I wanted to know what he said, and I wouldn't allow those words to leave me. He was a mystery but in a good way. Despite our interaction at first, he showed me kindness.

I watched as all the other girls counted their money for the night. Diamond and Kitten both had two thousand dollars. All the other girls made fifteen hundred. I hadn't looked at what the mystery man had given me. I didn't want to pull it out here because I knew it wouldn't be anything. It was a tip, but it wouldn't be nearly as much as the other girls made. I rolled my eyes and pulled it out of my boobs. I frowned when I noticed that it was a piece of paper.

Roxy walked back and laughed, "all you got was a piece of paper, pathetic."

Kitten walked over to me and rolled her eyes, "leave her alone."

I opened the paper quickly and my heart stopped in my chest. This wasn't just any piece of paper. It was a check, and the check was for ten-thousand-dollars.

Kitten grabbed it from me quickly, "damn baby doll. What the fuck, who gave you this?"

I put my hand on my chest and shook my head as the other girls gathered around. Kitten started to show them, and they were all shocked. Roxy was raging but I didn't care. Kitten handed me the check back and I stared down at it in disbelief.

"I don't know, he wouldn't give me his name."

Kitten patted me on the back, "well congrats. You deserve it!"

Roxy rolled her eyes, "who would give her a check? Come on, it's probably a bad check."

Sunny smiled, "no I don't think so. Men that were here tonight had money. There is no way that is a bad check."

Roxy shrugged, "maybe she did more for it. There is no way that a guy gave her that much money for passing out drinks."

Diamond sighed, "Roxy come on."

"I'm just being honest," she held her hands up in surrender.

"No, you're being a bitch again. Baby doll comes to work every Saturday and she never leaves with any money. Be happy for her this time, okay?" Diamond wrapped her arm around Roxy and shook her playfully.

I looked around, "I'll give you each one thousand dollars. I don't want to feel like I'm getting special treatment."

Candy laughed, "don't be silly. That's your money and you need to do what you want with it. We are not going to take away your blessing. Keep your money baby doll, we make that money every five days. We are not taking what you worked hard for."

I smiled and hugged her tightly, "thank you."

"What are we celebrating?" Everyone turned around when they heard Vain speak. His eyes locked with mine and I looked away quickly.

Roxy smiled, "oh nothing. Baby doll got a ten-thousand-dollar check tonight. We were just congratulating her on her new wealth."

I could sense Vain's anger from across the room. He smiled at the girls before he started clapping. "Everyone did well tonight. Will you girls give me a minute with baby doll please?"

They left the room quickly leaving me alone with Vain. I was scared and I didn't know why.

I did nothing wrong so there was no need to be scared. He walked towards me slowly and I sat up straight in my chair.

"You got a ten-thousand-dollar check?"

"Yes," I whispered.

He stopped in front of me, "who gave it to you?"

"I don't know, he wouldn't give me his name."

He grabbed a fistful of my hair quickly and pulled hard. "Don't lie to me. Who gave it to you and what did you do for it? Did you have sex in my club for that money?"

I frowned, "no. I wouldn't do that. I'm telling you the truth Vain. I didn't do anything wrong."

He pulled me up by my hair and shoved me against my makeup vanity. My back connected with the corner, and I screamed. He was yelling at me telling me to tell him the truth. The only thing I could do was sob loudly and plead with him. I didn't know why he was doing this. He was treating me like he hated me, and I couldn't understand why.

"VAIN PLEASE I'M NOT LYING...YOU'RE HURTING ME!"

He threw me on the ground roughly, "I want a name and I want it now."

I shook my head and crawled into the corner, "I don't know...please I don't know."

Vain stepped closer to me and I held my hands up in surrender. I couldn't take any more abuse from him.

"VAIN SHE IS TELLING THE TRUTH!" Kitten ran in and stared at him. He turned to face her, and she stood her ground. "I saw baby doll sitting at the table with the guy. She didn't do anything with him. They sat together for five minutes and then he left. I watched him tuck something in her breasts and I thought it was cash. She never left with him or touched him.

Sunny ran in and stood by Kitten, "I watched

from the stage. She was sitting with a guy and when I looked up again, he was walking away. She never left with him."

He walked out of the room leaving me alone with Sunny and Kitten. My body was trembling so badly that I couldn't control it. They ran over to me and tried to comfort me but all I could do was cry.

Confession

I couldn't face Vain after what he did to me. He hasn't called or text me since Saturday. I was fine with that anyway. I stared at the bruise on my back and sighed. I would have to wait for this to heal before I wore crop tops. I lifted my shirt down and walked towards the bathroom. I needed a shower and I needed it now. The hot water always made me feel better in a strange way. I grabbed my towel and walked towards the bathroom to start my water. I grabbed my phone and looked down at the text message that Kitten sent to me. She was checking on me every day since that situation happened with

Vain. She was shocked because she said that he never treated them like that. He was our protector, but he attacked me that night. She was thinking about not working for him anymore, but she was still thinking about it. I told her that I didn't want her to lose the way that she made money because of me. I knew that she cared about me but Vain was mad at me, not her. Anything that he did to me was personal, but I couldn't tell her that. I walked into the bathroom and closed the door. As much as I hated thinking about Vain, I couldn't stop. I fell in love with him, and I hated it. I had no business being around him, but I continued. I blamed myself for taking that stupid deal with him, but I was desperate. I didn't know what to do anymore because he wouldn't let me go. I turned on the shower and waited until the water was hot enough for me. I stripped and stepped in quickly. I sighed in relief when the water hit my skin. This is just what I needed to make me feel good. I smiled and stood under the running water as it poured over my face. Feeling the

warm water run through my hair was like
heaven. I opened my eyes slowly and stared
down at my feet. I had to do something about
this. I wasn't about to allow Vain to abuse me
and still work for him. I couldn't be near him
anymore and I had to tell him that. I didn't care
anymore about his threats. I wanted to get away
from him and there was no more stalling for
time. I wouldn't spend six months with him
treating me this way. He had no right to put his
hands on me. He did that while all the other
girls were standing outside the door. They
heard me scream and they heard him shove me
into the makeup vanity. It was embarrassing
and I couldn't seem to face anyone after that.
Diamond tried to comfort me, but she had no
luck. She kept telling me that Vain had been
drinking and he wasn't in his right mind. But
those were just excuses and she knew that. He
wanted to hurt me, and I didn't know why. He
was angry when he approached me, and he
knew that he was going to hurt me. That is why
he asked the other girls to leave. I sighed and

turned the shower water off. I needed to take a walk to clear my head. I grabbed my towel and stepped out of the tub wrapping it around myself. I pulled open the door and stepped into my bedroom. I jumped back when I realized that Roman was sitting on my bed. He looked like he was deep in thought, which was weird.

"Roman, are you okay?"

He looked up at me and shook his head, "you have been lying to me."

I frowned, "what do you mean?"

He stood up slowly, "don't play dumb with me. Why the hell are you working at a strip club? Why are you working for Vain Grey?"

My heart was pounding in my chest because I couldn't figure out how he knew. What was going on? Should I be honest, or should I continue to lie? I cleared my throat and tried to walk past him, "I don't know what you're talking about."

"CUT THE FUCKING LIES ATHENA. I
SWEAR TO GOD I'M NOT IN THE MOOD."

I stopped and turned to face him slowly. Roman
barely raised his voice when it came to me. I
knew that he was pissed off and me lying was
going to make him madder. I don't know how
he knew but he did. The best thing for me to do
was to come clean.

"What do you want?" I whispered.

"I want to know what the fuck is going on. I
want to know why a blonde-haired woman just
knocked on our door talking about baby doll
left her bag. I asked her who the hell is baby
doll and then she said your real name. She said
that baby doll is what they call you down there
at club Grey. I didn't believe her at first but
then she handed me your fucking bag." He
threw it at me, and I flinched as it hit me.

I balled my hands into fists tightly. I could feel
my blood boiling at this point. I was pissed off
at Roman because I wouldn't be in this position

if he would have given me the money I needed.

"You want the truth?"

"Yes, I want to know what the hell is going on." He sat down on my bed and ran his fingers through his hair roughly.

"I've been working for Vain for two and a half months now. He let me get the dance studio on credit and I agreed to work for him for six months. Every Saturday I go to his club and pass out drinks to the men."

He stood up slowly and walked towards me, "you've been working for Vain? Vain Grey? YOU CAN'T BE SERIOUS? OR ARE YOU JUST THAT DAMN STUPID ATHENA."

"This would have never happened if you would have given me the money in the first place! I would have never done any of this. But you were too busy having sex with Tarma to pay for my future."

He laughed, "cut the crap, okay? Stop blaming

me for the embarrassment that you caused our family. You keep saying I didn't give you the money but you're failing to realize that I didn't have to."

"What do you want me to say, huh? I'm sorry Roman, okay? I'm sorry that I lied to you and worked with your enemy." I shook my head and walked into the closet to get dressed. I grabbed a pair of panties and slid them on. I grabbed a blue maxi dress off the hanger and pulled it over my head. I knew that Roman still wanted to talk and I couldn't hide. I walked out of the closet to see him sitting on my bed.

"When did you meet him?"

I sat down on my desk, "I lied to you and went out with Tarma to a club two months ago. I didn't know that it was his club and that is where I met him. He popped up a week later and offered me the dance studio that he owned. I didn't know that he owned it until he told me."

"So, you took his offer? You didn't even think about what you were doing to the family name did you?"

I looked at him and sighed, "I didn't think that you would ever give me the money."

"Did you have sex with him? Don't lie to me because I will ask him."

I didn't want to answer that question. I couldn't give him the answer that he was looking for. That was going to set him over the top. There was no way that he would be able to control himself. I covered my face with my hand and shook my head.

"Roman," I whispered feeling the tears slid down my cheeks. I knew that he was going to feel embarrassed and betrayed.

"Did you have sex with him, yes or no?"

I sobbed softly covering my face with my hands. "Yes, but I can explain."

He stood up and punched the wall, "REALLY

YOU CAN EXPLAIN? GO AHEAD THEN, EXPLAIN."

"Roman I was hurt by what you did to me with Tarma. I wanted to get away from you and so I left with him. I didn't think that it was going to go that far. I was just trying to get away from you and the pain I felt. I felt betrayed by you, and I always obeyed you and you abused my trust."

"ATHENA, YOU DON'T GET MAD AT ME AND GO BE MY ENEMY'S WHORE! ARE YOU DUMB? YOU CAN'T SIT HERE AND TELL ME THAT."

I stood up, "YOU SHOULD HAVE NEVER HAD SEX WITH MY BEST FRIEND. YOU HURT ME ROMAN. YOU NEVER INVESTED IN MY DREAMS OR SUPPORTED ME."

"WHY SUPPORT SOMETHING THAT IS USELESS. YOU BELONG IN THE FUCKING MAFIA ATHENA. YOU THINK

YOU CAN LIVE A NORMAL LIFE BUT
YOU CAN'T." He yelled walking closer to me.

"YOU DON'T GET TO DECIDE MY
FUTURE!" I yelled shoving him away from
me.

I knew that he was upset but he was taking this
too far. I was not about to sit here and be yelled
at. Yes, what I did was wrong but if he
supported me, I wouldn't have to do it.

He closed his eyes and sighed, "you're right. To
be honest, you are no longer a sister of mine.
You'll be eighteen in six days and when that
day comes, I want you to leave. You can go be
his whore because I don't want a whore for a
sister."

I wiped away my tears quickly, "you can't be
serious? You're going to put me out of the
house?"

He walked towards my bedroom door, "yes.
You need to get out and go stay with him. You
chose to betray this family and so you are no

longer a part of it. Yea, I might have fucked
your friend, but I would never embarrass my
mother and father. You disgraced everything
they worked for. They wanted no parts of the
Grey family and now he has your virginity." He
walked out of my bedroom and slammed the
door. I couldn't believe what I was hearing. I
sank to my knees and sobbed softly. I didn't
know where I was going to go. Vain didn't care
about me and now my brother didn't care about
me. I could hear the front door open and close
and that's when I knew that he had left. I
expected him to be upset but not this upset.

I grabbed my phone and pressed the call button
under Kitten's name. I waited patiently for her
to pick up. She picked up on the second ring
and hearing her voice made me cry harder.

"Baby doll are you okay?"

"Yes, I don't know what to do. I-I don't know
what just happened Kitten."

"Baby calm down and tell me what happened.

Are you okay? Are you in a safe place? Did
someone hurt you?"

I took a deep breath, "my brother and I had a
big fight. He is putting me out of the house in
six days."

I heard her curse under her breath, "why?"

"Because Roxy came by and gave him the bag
that I left. She told him everything and he
didn't know about me working."

"Oh, I see. Damn, I'm going to kick her ass." I
heard her sigh loudly.

"What do I do? I don't have anywhere to go
Kitten. I really messed up and I wish that I
could take it all back."

I could hear her crying silently, "it's okay.
Trust me, we will get through it. I know that he
is upset but he can't stay mad at you. Listen, if
he wants you out then you can come and stay
with me. I won't let you just stay on the street;
you know I got your back."

"Thank you, but I don't want to take up extra space. I can stay at a hotel for a few days with the money I made." I smiled, "can you take me to a hotel? I can't stay in this house alone like this."

"Sure, we can have a movie night. I'll come to pick you up just give me fifteen minutes and I'll be over."

I said yes and she ended the call. I knew that running away wasn't going to fix this, but I didn't want to be here. I grabbed a bag and started to pack what I needed. I was going to leave just like he asked. In six days, I was going to come back and get my bank account information. I wanted the money that mom and dad left for me, and I would start my life with it. I didn't need Roman, and he was going to see that.

Birthday Girl

For the past few days, I have been staying in a hotel room. Roman hasn't text me or called me since the last time we spoke. Today was my birthday and I was excited. I was eighteen and finally an adult. Kitten planned a birthday dinner for me tonight. I didn't really feel up to it, but I promised her that I would show up. I stared at my reflection in the mirror and smiled. I looked sexy today and I needed to feel sexy. I checked my lipstick to make sure that it was still neat and in place. The last thing I needed was my outfit to look nice and then my makeup

ruined the whole look. I grabbed my black
heels and slid them on my feet. I was running a
little behind schedule, so I needed to leave now.
I grabbed my purse and the key to my hotel
room and walked towards the door. I checked
to make sure that I had everything and pulled
the door open. The hotel that I was staying at
was very nice and expensive. I was comfortable
here for the most part and that was good. I
walked down the quiet hallway and smiled.
Today was going to be a good day, I would
make sure of it. Before I went to the restaurant,
I had to stop at my house. I needed to get my
bank account information from Roman. I didn't
care to talk to him, but I knew I had to if I
wanted my money. He was going to give me a
difficult time about it, but he needed to get over
it. He already kicked me to the curb, the least
he could do is let me go in peace. I walked into
the elevator and pressed the button to go down.
My heart was pounding, and I was nowhere
near my house. I would have to take a taxi to
get there but I didn't mind. In a weird way, I

felt like a normal girl. Taking taxis and having
friends over was nice. Being able to go out and
not explain where I'm going. Not having
security lurking around watching me. It was too
good to be true sometimes. At first, I hated it
but then I realized that I was finally a normal
girl. I still went to my dance studio and
practiced even though my crew was gone.
Dancing always took away my stress and that
was the one thing I could always count on. I
stepped into the lobby of the hotel and walked
towards the door. Kitten was texting me telling
me to meet her in two hours. I needed to hurry
because she was going to kill me if I was late.

I unlocked the front door and stepped inside the
house. I could hear the tv and that is when I
knew that Roman was here. I walked into the
kitchen and there he was. He was fixing himself
something to eat in his Spongebob pajama
pants. I shook my head and smirked walking

over to the barstool. He didn't notice me until
he turned around.

"Hey," I smiled taking a seat.

He didn't say a word to me. He placed his food
on his plate and walked over to the refrigerator.
It had been six days and I thought that he would
be in a better mood, but I guess not.

"I'm here to get my bank account information.
I'll start moving my bed and stuff out by the
end of this week."

He looked at me and raised an eyebrow,
"you're not staying with your boyfriend."

I looked down at my hands, "he isn't my
boyfriend. I don't talk to him anymore; his
abuse is something I can't handle." I looked up
and shrugged taking a deep breath.

He frowned, "did he put his hands on you?"

I sighed, "I don't want to cry because I'll ruin
my makeup." I tried to laugh but it came out as
a soft sob. I never talked about the abuse I

endured from Vain. I felt embarrassed and
ashamed that I loved someone like that. I fell in
love with a man who didn't want to love me but
use me. It was embarrassing and I was dumb
for staying with him.

He walked over to me and grabbed my hand,
"tell me the truth."

"He um…he hurt me a lot. I never wanted to
betray you and I tried to get away from him. I
never wanted this to happen. I made a mistake
and I regretted it every day. I wanted to tell you
so bad, but I was scared. I was scared that you
would hate me. I knew that you would never
look at me the same. I tried to pay him off with
the check that you gave me, but he wouldn't
take it. I know that I should have told you, but I
was scared."

He grabbed me and pulled me into a hug, "I'm
going to kill him."

I sobbed loudly and clung to my brother. I
needed to feel his arms around me. I needed to

feel protected because I haven't lately. I've been going through all this by myself, and I needed Roman. I hated that I was living this double life. I wanted to be close to my brother again. He was the only family that I had, and I couldn't let that go. I knew that he was still going to be mad at me, but I didn't care. I needed him more than he knew right now.

He pulled away from, "Athena, I know that I can be hard to talk to. But you don't keep things like this from me. You could have been hurt and I would have never known what happened to you. I love you and I regret everything I said a few days ago. I was angry and I felt defeated because I wanted to protect you."

"You do protect me," I whispered wiping my nose.

He shook his head, "no I don't. Vain has had his eyes on you for a year. I have gotten threats from him saying that he was going to hurt you. He went as far as to say that he would kill you if I didn't give him my part of the city. His goal was to have sex with you. I tried to stop that from happening because I knew that he just wanted to use you. That is why I flipped out when I heard about Tarma dealing with Ace. In the end, it didn't matter. He got what he wanted and now he will always have that to throw in my face. Just thinking about it makes my blood boil." He balled up his fists and leaned against the counter.

I couldn't believe what I was hearing. Meeting Vain was not an accident at all. He did all this on purpose just to have something over my brother. I felt so damn stupid because I actually thought he cared about me. It was all a lie, and he knew that. That is why he has been treating me the way he has these past few days. He was done with me, and he didn't want to say it.

"I'm sorry I didn't know."

He sighed, "it's not your fault. I should have been honest with you about what was going on. I couldn't bring myself to scare you like that.

You were finally living a normal life. You went to a normal high school and met normal people. How could I dump mafia stuff on you like that? You made it very clear that you didn't want anything to do with it. I tried to let you live the normal life you wanted."

I pulled him into a hug, "I love you."

He hugged me back, "I love you too. I don't want you to move out, but I can't stop you. You're eighteen today and you can make your own decisions."

I smiled, "I got accepted into college in Chicago. I was hoping that maybe I could go. I'll come back for the summer and holidays; I promise."

He laughed, "if that is what you want. You look pretty today, where are you going?"

"A friend of mine planned birthday dinner. Do you want to come?" I giggled grabbing his hand.

"No thanks, I would rather do something with you alone. I'll plan something for us to do tomorrow. Does that sound like a plan?"

I stood up and wrapped my arms around him. "Yes, that sounds perfect. I have to go but I'll see you tonight, okay? Maybe we can watch a movie."

He smiled, "I'll be waiting. By the way, Happy birthday. I got you a gift to add a cherry on top of the cake."

I laughed, "what is it?"

"Well, I got you two gifts. The first gift is the termination of your contract with Vain. I got a lawyer and he discovered that the contract was a violation of the law. You were underage at the time the contract was signed and reviewed. The second gift is this," he pulled a necklace from behind his back.

My eyes widened when I realized that it was my moms' necklace. My father gave it to her when they first met, and she wore it for ten years. She never took it off and she cherished it. I turned around so Roman could put it on me. It was a gold necklace with a beautiful gold butterfly pendant. The wings of the butterfly were covered in diamonds. I placed my hand on the necklace and smiled.

"Thank you," I whispered placing a kiss on his cheek.

"He hugged me tight one last time, "get going before you're late."

I nodded my head and ran towards the door. He was right, if I was late Kitten was going to kill me.

"HAPPY BIRTHDAY TO YOU…HAPPY BIRTHDAY TO YOU…HAPPY BIRTHDAY, ATHENA…HAPPY BIRTHDAY TO YOU!"

I shook my head and hid my face as Kitten sang loudly. I was grateful that we were outside so that she couldn't embarrass me. She laughed and passed me a piece of cake and I sat back in my chair rubbing my stomach.

"I can't eat another bite," I whined.

"Don't be a baby," she laughed licking her fingers.

I rolled my eyes and looked down at my phone. It was getting late, and I promised Roman a movie night. I hated to leave so early but I needed to get home.

"Hey, I'm going to head home. I promised my brother I would spend time with him."

She pouted, "aww but the drinks are about to come."

I laughed and hugged her, "you drink enough for me. You girls get home safe, okay?"

They all said yes and waved me goodbye as I walked away from them. I didn't want to break my promise to Roman. We just got back on good terms, and I wanted to keep things that way. Besides I wanted to spend time with him on my special day. I walked down the sidewalk and looked up at the night sky. It was so beautiful here in the city and I loved it. Even though New York was crowded, I wouldn't change living here for anything.

"You look beautiful."

I stopped and turned around when I heard Vain speak to me. He was standing behind me in a suit and tie. He looked handsome tonight, but I didn't want to see him. I didn't understand why he was here.

"What do you want?"

He stepped closer to me, and I stepped back, "don't come any closer. I swear to God I will call the police. Whatever you have to say, you can say from right there."

"You owe me," he smirked.

"I owe you nothing. You need to leave me alone and stay the hell away from me."

"Your brother interfered with our contract so now you have to make up for it. What are you going to offer me now?"

"A knife in the heart if you keep stalking me." I balled my hands into fists.

He held his hands up in surrender, "why are you so upset? Are you mad that I didn't love you back? Are you upset that I didn't fuck you more than I did? Or are you upset that I got bored with you and moved on?"

I smirked, "if that is the case why are you here now? If you moved on and you didn't love me then you wouldn't be following me. You're mad that I don't want you and I never will Vain. You can go to hell," I whispered turning around and walking away.

To my surprise, he didn't follow me. I wasn't in the mood for his bullshit tonight and I wasn't going to stand for his abuse. I continued to walk home in order to catch my brother for the movie tonight.

Roman

I grabbed my phone and stared at the unfamiliar number calling me. I didn't want to answer but something inside me told me to. I had been calling Athena all night and she hasn't answered her phone. I woke up this morning and she still wasn't home. I sighed and pressed the answer button on the screen.

"Hello."

"Hey," a female's voice screamed in the phone. "Are you Roman?"

"Yes, who's asking?" I asked rolling my eyes.

"It's me, Kitten. I'm Athena's friend and I was

wondering if you've heard from her. I have been calling her all night and all morning and no answer."

I frowned, "I thought that she was with you."

"She was but she left early last night. She said that she was coming home to catch a movie with you. I haven't heard from her since."

"Look, I need to start doing some digging. I'll call you back as soon as I find something out." I ended the call quickly and grabbed my keys. I knew that Vain had something to do with this and I was going to fucking kill him. I knew where he was, and I was going to beat his ass once and for all.

I saw Vain standing by a park bench with some of his men. I didn't waste any time running up to him and punching him in his face. The punch took him off guard and he fell to the ground.

"WHERE THE FUCK IS SHE? WHERE IS MY SISTER!"

He stood up and tried to charge for me, but Ace held him back. I wanted to do more damage, but I knew that I needed to find Athena.

He growled, "I don't know what you're talking about. I haven't seen her since last night."

"Don't play with me Vain. Where is she? No one has heard from her, and she is not answering her phone."

He turned his back to me, "that sounds like a personal problem. She is no longer any concern of mine."

"SO, YOU CAN USE HER AND ABUSE HER BUT NOT CARE ABOUT HER?" He was proving just how heartless he was. I took a deep breath and turned to leave. There was no way that he was going to help me, and I knew that. I looked over and a girl sitting next to Ace smiled at me. I smiled back but my smile quickly faded when I saw that she was wearing the necklace that I had given Athena. I walked over to her and smiled before snatching the necklace off her neck.

"Where the hell did you get this? This necklace belongs to my sister."

She frowned, "I was walking down the street downtown and I saw it on the ground. I thought that it was something that was lost so I picked it up. There was a little bit of blood on it and the ground had droplets of blood too."

My heart stopped in my chest, "what?" I whispered.

"Which area downtown?" Ace asked standing up.

"Umm it was by the restaurant called the Golden Tail," she smiled.

Ace placed his hand on Vain's shoulder, "we need to find her. I know that you don't want to work with Roman but do it for Athena."

Vain hesitated but nodded his head, "okay. I'll help."

I raced towards my car quickly. I was going to find her if it was the last thing I did.

"Please be alive," I whispered starting the car.

ABOUT THE AUTHOR

Marsha was born in 1996 in Chicago. She has many hobbies including writing. She has been writing since she was thirteen years old. The beast within was her first published book and it was published in 2018. She loves Anime, exploring new places, and spending time with her daughter.

Printed in Great Britain
by Amazon